DOWN A STREET
THAT WASN'T
THERE

DOWN A STREET THAT WASN'T THERE

MARIE BRENNAN

First published 2020 by Book View Café Publishing Cooperative.
304 S. Jones Blvd. Ste# 2906
Las Vegas, Nevada 89107
http://bookviewcafe.com

Print edition 2021
ISBN 978-1-61138-965-4

"Coyotaje" was first published in *Bewere the Night*, ed. Ekaterina Sedia, April 2011. "Selection" was first published in *Electric Velocipede* #13, November 2007. "Such as Dreams Are Made Of" was first published in *Aberrant Dreams* #8, Summer 2006. "La Molejera" was first published in *Cirsova Magazine*, September 2019. "Comparison of Efficacy Rates for Seven Antipathetics as Employed Against Lycanthropes" was first published in *Running With the Pack*, ed. Ekaterina Sedia, April 2010. "The Last Wendy" was first published in *On Spec* # 81, Summer 2010. "The Genius Prize" was first published in *Kaiju Rising II: Reign of Monsters*, ed. N.X. Sharps and Alana Joli Abbott, November 2018.

CONTENTS

Foreword

There are five basic schools of thought on the topic of author commentary in a short story collection: 1) put it all together at the front; 2) all together at the back; 3) individually before each story; 4) individually after each story; and 5) don't bother.

For the ebook editions of these collections, I can leverage the format to facilitate multiple approaches, by linking to the notes at the end of each story while collecting the notes themselves at the end of the book. Alas, dead trees are not so flexible, which means I have to pick. You will find all the story notes following the Afterword, and can time your reading of them as you choose.

This collection contains seven stories, all of them set in our own modern world or a slightly futuristic version thereof, with some kind of speculative twist. I hope you enjoy them!

COYOTAJE

THE COYOTES OF MEXICALI were bold. They did their business in cantinas, in the middle of the afternoon; the police, well-fed with bribes, looked the other way. Day by day, week by week, people came into Mexicali, carrying backpacks and bundles and small children, and day by day, week by week, they went away again, vanishing while the back of the police was obligingly turned.

If the people could afford it. "The price is twenty-five thousand pesos," the coyote repeated, and drained the last of his beer. "If you can't pay, stop wasting my time."

Inés bit her lip, looking down at the scratched formica table-top. "I don't have twenty-five thousand. I only have—" She stopped herself before saying the number. Mexicali was far from the worst of the border towns, but it was bad enough, if you went looking for the wrong people.

The coyote shrugged. "Try El Rojo. He might take you for less. Especially if you have something else to offer." The quick downward flick of his eyes made his meaning clear.

"Where can I find El Rojo?"

"La Puerta del Oro, in Chinesca. Ask for shark-fin tacos."

Inés nodded and got up. She heard footsteps following her as she left the cantina, and whirled once she was through the door, prepared to defend herself.

Her pursuer held up his hands, letting the door swing shut behind him. "Relax. I only followed because I heard what Ortega said. Don't go to El Rojo."

The sun was like a hammer on Inés' back, trying to pound her into the dust. But it meant she could see the other man's face, broad and pocked with the occasional scar, seamed where he squinted against the light. "If he's cheaper, I have to. Nobody told me it would be this expensive."

The man—another coyote—shrugged and pulled sunglasses from his pocket. "Can't help it. With all the new laws, it's a lot riskier for us, and you need documents on the other side. Look, I'll take you for twenty."

Inés shook her head. "I don't have twenty, either."

"Then stay here a while. There's jobs—not good ones, but if you're patient you can save enough to get across. *Safely.* El Rojo... he isn't safe."

None of it was safe; even the honest coyotes could get a migrant killed. "I don't have any choice," she said.

With the man's eyes hidden by the sunglasses, she couldn't be sure, but she thought he gave her a pitying look. "Go with God, then. And be careful."

Caution had gone out the window when Javier died. Shading her eyes against the desert sun, Inés went in search of La Puerta de Oro.

It lay in Mexicali's Chinatown, its garish red and gold faded by the elements. The interior was blindingly dark, after the street outside. "Shark-fin tacos," she said once her eyes adjusted, and the hostess jabbed her thumb toward a table in the back corner.

Two men sat there, both facing the door. The bigger one grinned as Inés approached, licking his lips in an exaggerated gesture, but it was the skinnier one *she* watched. He had a predator's eyes.

She cast her gaze down when she got to the table. "I want to get across the border," she said. Quietly, but not whispering. "I heard El Rojo could take me."

"I can," the smaller man said. He was wiry more than slender, hardened to rawhide by the desert sun. Other Mexicali coyotes took migrants in secret truck compartments, sneaking them across into Calexico or up to State Route 7, then onward to San Diego or Phoenix. El Rojo, according to rumor, went a more dangerous route, through the Sonoran Desert. Less risk of being caught by the Border Patrol, but more risk of dying, whether from thirst or the guns of militia. Or coyotes, of the four-legged kind.

Inés sat, eyes still downcast. The last thing she wanted was for him to take her stare as a challenge. "I can pay ten thousand." The bigger fellow laughed, a barking sound in the quiet of the restaurant. "That and a bit more will do, girl," he said, laying one hand on her knee as if she might not catch his meaning.

She controlled her revulsion; pulling away too fast would make her look like prey. It was the other man who mattered, anyway. El Rojo, the red one. There were many possible explanations for the nickname, few of them reassuring.

His method of bargaining showed a sharp mind. From money, he would switch without warning to questions about Inés: where she was from, why she was emigrating, what kind of work she thought she would find. She told him she came from Cuauhtémoc in Chihuahua, and had a brother who crossed at Nogales two years ago; if she could get to Albuquerque, her brother knew a man who could get her a job as a maid. Seventeen thousand, El Rojo said, and if she was coming from Cuauhtémoc and going to Albuquerque, why had she come to Mexicali? A man had brought her this far, promising help, Inés said, but he'd tried to rape her; she would pay fifteen thousand and no more.

El Rojo smiled, thin, lips closed. "That'll do. Half now, half when we get there, and Pipo here will show you to your room."

"My room?" Inés asked, alarm rising in her throat.

Now he showed a glint of teeth. "I'm your coyote now. Full service, from here until your trip is done. Wouldn't want you getting picked up by the cops."

Or telling anybody about his business. This was his reputation, that he was shrewd and careful, and utterly without human morals. If she gave him reason to cut her throat, he would, without hesitation.

She'd hoped to send a letter, in case she didn't survive this trip. "Do you think I'm stupid? I didn't bring the money with me."

He gestured at his companion. "Pipo will go with you to fetch it. We have a deal, and until it's done, you're mine."

The 'room' Pipo showed her to was a basement elsewhere in Chinesca, though Inés, blindfolded, only knew it by the smell of spices. What sort of deals had El Rojo struck, that he chose to do business out of this part of Mexicali?

Maybe the police just paid less attention to the Chinese district. Certainly Pipo felt comfortable enough to lead her blindfolded through the streets, by a very roundabout path. When he shoved her off the last step and yanked off the bandanna, Inés found more than a dozen people in the basement already, sitting in the light of a single dim bulb, watching her with wary eyes.

"Tomorrow night," Pipo said, and left.

Inés brushed her hair from her face, nodded at the migrants, and found a place to sit by the wall, where she leaned against a broken piece of tabletop. Nobody spoke; she didn't expect it. Right now they were all strangers, in an unknown place, taking an enormous risk. Talk would come later, when shared trials created a sense of bonding; then she would hear about relatives on the other side of the border, or the hope of work—whatever dream or desperation sent them on this journey.

She studied them, though, out of the corners of her eyes, taking care never to stare at anyone. Most were a bit younger than her: in their teens, maybe early twenties. A few women, the rest men; three of the women were cradling children too young to walk. One man was substantially older—maybe his fifties, though with his face so wrinkled by the sun, she could be off by ten years. He made no pretense about not staring at her, though when Inés returned the look he glanced away, scratching his fingers through hair like grey wire.

Fifteen thousand pesos, Inés had promised El Rojo. Assume the same for everyone here; some maybe bargained better, some worse, and she didn't know if he charged the same for little kids.

Seventeen people in this basement, counting her. Assume that was average. Two hundred fifty-five thousand pesos—more than twenty thousand dollars. How often did El Rojo do this? Every month? Less often? More? However she did the math, *coyotaje* was a profitable business.

One for which many people paid the price.

Javier would've told Inés she was an idiot for coming here, for putting herself into El Rojo's hands. But Javier was gone, and she was the only one who could do this.

She lay down on the hard concrete and tried to get some sleep.

When the basement door slammed open, half the people there were already awake; within seconds, all of them were on their feet, and one mother stifled her daughter's wail. Pipo grinned at them, blunt face monstrous in the dim light, and jerked a thumb toward the door. "Time to go."

Inés sneaked a glance at her mother's old watch, with its extra hole punched in the band to fit her smaller wrist. An hour past sunset. They would make their move in the dead of night.

Last chance to run.

But it was a lie. She'd passed up that chance when she sat down at El Rojo's table—maybe when she came to Mexicali in search of him. Inés followed the others upstairs and into the narrow alley behind.

A truck waited there. Inés didn't see El Rojo, but three other men were helping Pipo, and one climbed into the back with the migrants before the door was rolled down and locked into place. No secret compartment, not here; this was only to get them out of town. Most of the journey would be done on foot.

More waiting, this time in near-total darkness. Inés sat with her backpack in the hollow of her crossed legs, arms wrapped around it, swaying into the grey-haired man or the young woman on the other side every time the truck slowed or accelerated or hit a rough patch of road. The young woman sat in much the same

position, only it was a little girl she held, a year old at most. The
infant, of course, didn't understand what was going on, and
burbled loudly to herself in the darkness.

"Shut her up, already," one of the young men said abruptly,
breaking the stifling silence that overlaid the noise of the truck.
"That brat's gonna get us caught."

Inés felt the mother shrink back in alarm. "Hey!" Inés said,
glaring into the darkness, as if the complainer could see her.
"She's happy. Would you rather she was crying?"

By the voice, she guessed him to be one of the younger
ones—probably the weedy kid, fifteen at most, and twitchy with
nerves. "I'd rather she shut up. Do you have any idea how far
noise like that's gonna carry, once we're out in the desert?"

Better than you do. Instead she answered, "Let her tire herself
out now; then she'll be quiet later. The hard part's still ahead of
us."

"Nobody asked you," the boy said, but it was sullen rather
than threatening. When nobody else spoke up in his support, he
made a disgusted sound and fell silent. The mother was stiff at
Inés' side, but she made no protest when Inés held her fingers out
blindly, for the baby to play with. A bump in the road sent her
backpack toppling from her lap, but an anonymous hand pushed
it back into place.

Some time after that, the truck slowed, turned, left the paved
road. Inés guessed they had been driving for maybe three hours;
presuming they were going east, that put them well past Yuma,
into the harsh desert of Sonora. So far, at least, the rumors were
true.

Knowing still didn't prepare her for what greeted the migrants
when the truck rattled to a halt and Pipo let them out. All around
was hard dirt and scrub brush, blue and grey beneath the brilliant
canopy of the stars. Inés found herself suddenly, irrationally
reluctant to leave the truck; it was the only human thing in sight,
and once it was gone, they would be completely at the mercy of
the coyotes.

Where is El Rojo?

He appeared without warning, from what Inés would have sworn was an empty patch of desert. The coyote sauntered toward them, hands comfortably in his pockets, but she wasn't fooled by the show of relaxation; the wary grace of his movement said he was very much alert. "Any trouble?" he asked.

Pipo bent to murmur in his ear. Inés, straining to hear, caught a scrap about the baby. El Rojo's lip curled in annoyance, and her muscles tensed. But the mother had paid, and a coyote who abandoned his cargo too easily would soon get a reputation that destroyed future business. He waved Pipo back, and turned his attention to the waiting group.

"Listen carefully," he told them, in a quiet voice that raised the hairs on Inés' neck, "because anybody who dies from not paying attention won't be my problem.

"We're going over the fence. Pipo and the boys will show you how. Anybody who makes a sound while we're climbing over will pay for it. Anybody who hesitates gets left behind. When I run, you run until I stop. Anybody who can't keep up, gets left behind. We'll go until midday, rest for four hours, move again. I say 'quiet,' you shut up or pay for it. I say 'hide,' you go straight for the nearest cover, get low, don't move until I tell you. Me and the boys leave, you stay where you are, unless you feel like dying. I give you any other orders, you obey, and don't ask questions. Got it?"

He waited until every migrant had nodded. Nobody dared make a sound, not even to say yes. When he had agreement, El Rojo said, "Let's go."

The fence was a black scar across the desert's face, looming high overhead. No cameras or lights out here, Inés knew, unless vigilantes on the other side had installed their own—but she trusted El Rojo to be canny enough to know if they had. Didn't trust the man any further than that, but to be competent at his business, yes. He had a good system for crossing, too. Pipo made a cup of his hands and lifted his boss to the top of the wall, where El Rojo balanced easily and unfurled a rope ladder, which one of the other men staked down in the dirt. It seemed considerate, until Inés saw how much more quickly people climbed, not having to rappel; and the ladder was more portable than a rigid one, less permanent than a tunnel. It fit everything she knew about him: quick, simple, and above all, efficient.

It was hardest for the women with small children. Mindful of El Rojo's warning, Inés held out her hands wordlessly; after a moment's hesitation, the mother she'd been sitting next to handed over her daughter, then climbed the ladder. When she was at the top, Inés stretched up to give the sleepy infant back. Then she did the same for the other two, quickly soothing the one baby who looked likely to fuss. Pipo glared, but said nothing.

She was the last one over, except for the coyotes. Not letting herself hesitate, Inés balanced on the swaying rope ladder and scrambled up to the top. With her hands braced on the fence's edge, she swung one leg over—and there she paused.

One foot in each world. It felt like it should mean something, like this fence, this barrier dividing one nation from its neighbor, should mark some profound transition. It didn't. The desert on the far side looked no different. It was all borderland, and its inhabitants, regardless of nation, had more in common with each other than with those who lived inside. She had always stood with one foot in each world; only now it was literally true.

Inés swung her other leg over and dropped to the ground below. Now she was just another illegal immigrant, risking her life to enter the United States.

As soon as she landed, El Rojo began to run.

Across the hard-packed stripe of the border road, through the scrubby bushes beyond, not waiting for the coyotes to pack up the ladder and climb down after them. They, Inés supposed, would catch up soon. The pace El Rojo set was steady, but not too fast; they would be at this for a while. She settled her backpack on her shoulders and relaxed into her stride.

The ones with children had it worst. Inés hung back, trying with her presence to give them support; it was easier to run in company than alone. The baby girl she'd played with in the truck, jolted into unhappy wakefulness, started to wail, and the mother clapped a desperate hand over her daughter's mouth. Inés tensed, looking at El Rojo, but it seemed the order against noise had only applied at the fence.

Or perhaps the paying would come later.

She worried about the older man, too. This would be a hard enough journey for her, and she was young, fit, and used to the trials of the desert. How much worse would it be for him? But the man had energy enough to spare her a rueful smile as he ran. Inés wondered what his story was. Everyone who crossed the border had one.

Running, running through the night, El Rojo in the lead, and Inés fixed her gaze on his back, as if he were prey she would wear down and finally catch.

By the time they slowed to a walk, many of the migrants were gasping. Everyone reached for water; the less cautious gulped theirs, thinking only of immediate thirst, and not the miles of desert that still lay ahead. Inés sipped cautiously, trying to estimate how far they'd come. Two miles from the border? To the left, the ground rose in a thin, jagged line. The Sierra Pinta, if she was reading their location right. El Rojo would take them through the San Cristobel wash and south of Ajo Peak, to the Tohono O'odham reservation. The people there had rescued more than a few migrants from death in the desert. Not all of those they rescued were reported to the Border Patrol, either; the Tohono O'odham knew what it was like be split apart by a fence. Some of their kin lived on the other side.

They got a short break at sunrise, among a scattering of saguaro that would hide them from distant eyes. Inés took a hat from her bag, then slipped her hand back in, hunting by touch, until she found the rubber-banded tin tucked inside her one clean shirt. She waited until the coyotes were looking elsewhere, then shifted the tin into her pocket, where she could reach it more quickly.

A scuff of foot against stone made her jump. The older man held up calming hands, then crouched at her side and murmured, "Miguel."

"Inés," she murmured back, keeping a wary eye on the coyotes.

"You seem well prepared."

The practiced lie rose easily to her lips. "My brother crossed a few years ago. Gave me some advice."

He smiled. "Brothers are like that."

Eduardo *had* given her advice, when she showed up on his doorstep in Cuauhtémoc. Much of it had involved swearing. Not that he doubted what Inés had to say; Mother had once sent him out into the desert, too, as she had later done with Inés. But he thought she should let it go. Or let someone else take care of it— as if that had done any good yet.

And she owed Javier too much to let it go.

"If an old man can give you advice, too," Miguel said, even quieter than before, "watch out for that one." He made a tiny gesture toward El Rojo. "He's got his eye on you. But not in the usual way."

Inés' fingers tightened on her backpack. "What do you mean?"

Miguel shook his head. "I don't know. The big one, he wants what you'd expect, but the leader...he's watching you for something."

For what, Inés wanted to ask—but El Rojo rose smoothly to his feet, and they had to follow. It wasn't a question Miguel could likely answer, anyway.

With the sun now up, the desert rapidly heated from pleasantly cool to sweltering. Inés and Miguel both took turns carrying the small children, to give their mothers a rest. Why were they crossing now, in the brutal conditions of summer? Couldn't they wait for milder weather? She bit back the desire to yell at the mothers for stupidity. She didn't know their reasons. And it would upset the kids, who out of all those here were completely blameless. Not that innocence would save them, if immigration agents caught their families; they would be deported back to Mexico, with or without their parents.

Inés gritted her teeth and kept walking.

When the noon halt came, people sank down wherever they stood, trembling and drenched with sweat. El Rojo wandered among them, cursing and kicking, until everyone was as hidden as they could get. Even in this desolation, they couldn't assume they would remain unnoticed; the so-called Minutemen rode through here on their self-appointed patrols, and some of them were far too ready to shoot.

Miguel joined Inés in her clump of creosote. The bushes didn't offer much in the way of shelter, not with the sun directly overhead, but it was all they had. The older man offered her beef jerky; Inés gave him chips in exchange, wishing she had brought more. They made her thirsty, but it was necessary to replace the salt lost through sweat, and she could tell that few of the migrants had known to bring their own. She hoped they found a cache of water left by one of the humanitarian groups; some people hadn't brought enough.

Murmurs rose here and there as people made brief conversation, then gave it up out of exhaustion. One curt order, though, made Inés stiffen: El Rojo, speaking to the mother whose daughter had fussed the most. "Come with me."

Miguel's hand clamped down on Inés' arm before she could move. "Don't."

"I can't let him—" Inés growled, trying to rise. El Rojo was leading the young woman to the far side of a cluster of ocotillo.

"Yes, you can," Miguel hissed. "Look." He jerked his chin; Inés, following, saw Pipo watching her. *He wants what you'd expect,* Miguel had said—what El Rojo was about to take from that woman. *Something else to offer,* the coyote in the cantina had said. For all she knew, this was part of the woman's bargain with El Rojo. Which didn't make it right, didn't make it okay—

You aren't here to rescue them, Inés. Not like that. Don't forget your purpose.

She sagged back down, defeated, and tried to sleep. It wasn't the heat and relentless sun that kept her awake, though, but the muffled sounds from nearby.

They rested through the hottest part of the day, then rose to walk some more. Now it was clear that, however hard the night and morning had been, that was only the beginning of their trials; stiff muscles protested, and weariness made everyone clumsy.

One of the young men stumbled on his way down a slope, nearly falling, putting Inés' heart in her mouth; if he twisted an ankle, he was dead. Nobody would carry him, not all the way to the reservation. He regained his balance, unharmed, and they went on.

Until the sun set and the desert air cooled, and Inés, stupid with exhaustion, began to wonder if all this risk and effort was going to come to nothing whatsoever, except an embarrassed trek back to Phoenix, and a passport in her mailbox with no stamp marking her return to the United States. *It isn't nothing,* she thought, *you know about El Rojo now, and can tell—*

"*Hide,*" the coyote snarled.

The migrants didn't move fast enough. They'd been stumbling along, one foot in front of the other, like zombies, and now they stared at him; Pipo and the others began shoving people to the ground as distant headlights sliced through the thickening dusk.

Inés remained standing, staring, until Pipo knocked her down, almost into the spines of an ocotillo. Two lights, moving independently: all-terrain motorcycles, not a Jeep. Border Patrol, not vigilantes, and following their trail from the fence.

A low, quiet laugh from El Rojo raised all the hairs along her arms and neck. "Come on, boys."

Making only a little more noise than the desert wind, he and his three fellows loped off toward the approaching motorcycles.

Inés shoved a hand into her pocket, pulling out the rubber-banded tin. When she rose to a crouch, Miguel whispered, "What are you doing?" He wasn't close enough to grab her.

Keeping those agents alive. "Stay here," she hissed back, and ran before he could protest.

She kept low, taking advantage of the scant cover. Already she'd lost sight of El Rojo and the others, but that wouldn't matter for long. She just needed to get far enough away from the migrants…

Good enough. Inés dropped to one knee, stripped out of her clothes, and pulled the rubber band off the tin.

The pungent smell of the *teopatli* inside rose into the dry air. Its scent brought memories swarming around her like ghosts: her first visit to Cuauhtémoc, at the age of fifteen, re-united after seven years with the family she had lost. Her mother sending her out into the desert, with *teopatli* for her skin and pulque to drink and a maguey thorn to pierce her tongue, as her ancestors had done for generations before.

Careful despite her haste, Inés dipped her fingers in the paste, and began to dab it onto her body. Legs, back, arm, face, rings and clusters of spots, and even before she was done she could feel the *ololiuqui* seeds ground into the paste taking effect. Her vision swam, going both blurry and sharp, and smells assaulted her nose. Then everything came together with a bone-wrenching snap, and leaving tin and clothes behind, Inés ran once more.

The coyotes weren't hard to follow now. They feared no predators, out here in the desert; Border Patrol, vigilantes, ranchers, all were just different kinds of prey. The coyotes ran together for a time, then fanned out, and Inés went after the nearest, knowing she would have to be fast.

He was on his way up a steep rise, aiming for a cliff from which he could leap. Inés caught him halfway, slamming his wiry body to the ground, her jaws seeking and then finding his skull, teeth punching through into his brain. The coyote died without a sound, as in the distance, the barking calls of his brothers pierced the night air.

The motorcycles growled lower at the sound, but they were still approaching much too fast. Inés ran again, the *teopatli* giving her strength she'd lacked before. She was made for the stalking ambush, not the chase, but the lives of those two agents depended on her speed. The second coyote died with his throat crushed. The noise dropped sharply; one of the engines had stopped. She caught the third coyote on his way toward the motorcycles, and this one saw her coming; he twisted away from her leap, yipping in surprise, before going down beneath her much greater weight.

Even as the hot blood burst into her mouth, she heard a scream from the direction of the engines—a human scream.

Cold blue light flooded the narrow valley where the migrants had walked. One of the motorcycles had fallen on its side; the rider lay moaning and bleeding. His partner had a shotgun out, and was pointing it in every direction, unsure where the next attack would come from. If Inés wasn't careful, he would shoot her instead.

Now it was time for the stalk. She circled the area slowly, paws touching down with silent care, nose alive to every scent on the wind. She thought the third coyote had been Pipo—couldn't be sure—but the last was El Rojo. He was the smart one, the subtle one, the sorcerer who had given them all coyote shape, the better to hunt the humans who came to hunt them.

He knew she was out here. Inés realized that when she found his trail looping upon itself, confusing his scent. He'd heard Pipo die, of course—but maybe he'd known since before then. *He's watching you for something,* Miguel had said. Maybe El Rojo recognized a fellow sorcerer when he saw one.

On an ordinary night, she wouldn't have been stupid enough to approach the overhang. But the strength the *teopatli* gave her was no substitute for sleep; Inés' human mind was sluggish, ceding too much control to the beast.

A weight crashed into her back. Pain bloomed hot along her nerves as the coyote's jaws closed on her neck. Acting on instinct, Inés collapsed and rolled, dislodging El Rojo. When she regained her feet, she saw at last the creature she had come all this way to hunt.

His coat was different than the others', more uniform in color along the head and back. In sunlight, it would be reddish brown. El Rojo, the red one, whose jaws now dripped red with her blood. Who had murdered Javier, and Consuela, and David, ranchers and vigilantes, and probably some migrants, too. Coyote attacks, the official reports said; they were suddenly more common than before. But agents of the Border Patrol died more often in the line of duty than any other federal law enforcement division, and the people in charge were more concerned with human killers than animal attacks.

Only Inés suspected more. She could hardly tell anyone it was *nagualismo*, though, even if she admitted to being a *nagual* herself. And so she had gone south, into Mexico, returning as an illegal immigrant, to hunt the coyote who ran on both two legs and four. They snapped and feinted at one another, El Rojo using his greater speed and agility. But that was a dangerous game for him to play, especially on his own; when coyotes hunted larger prey, they did so in packs, and his was dead. That was why he had ambushed her—and as if he remembered that at the same moment, El Rojo turned and ran.

Inés followed. It might be enough to have killed the others, or it might not. If he could share his *nagualismo* with anyone, it wouldn't take him long to be back in business. But it wasn't pragmatism that drove her; it was the memory of Javier's funeral, and his sister's grief. And her own devastated face, staring back at her from the mirror.

The beast wanted his blood.

And the beast was stupid, forgetting she wasn't the only predator out here tonight. The shotgun blast clipped her right hip, a few of the pellets raking bloody tracks into her fur. El Rojo had lured her back toward the motorcycles, and the agent with the gun. That man didn't know she was a friend. Inés roared, and leaped out of range.

Bleeding, trembling with exhaustion even the *teopatli* couldn't erase, she prayed, as she'd once prayed to the spirit of the day on which she was born. Alone in the desert, hallucinating and exhausted, bleeding from the tongue in the old manner, she'd begged the spirit to come—and the jaguar had answered.

El Rojo was creeping up behind her, not quite silent enough. Inés waited, paws braced against the rocky dirt. Closer. And closer.

When he leapt, she twisted to meet him, with all the speed and power of the jaguar.

One massive paw slammed him to the side. El Rojo yelped, but it cut off as her jaws found his neck. With a single bite, she severed his spinal cord, and his body went limp in the dust.

Panting, she stood over the body of her prey. Not far away,

she heard the second engine start up again, and the crunching rush of the motorcycles driving away. The wounded agent was well enough to ride, then, and they'd given up the chase.

For now.

Inés licked her spotted fur clean as best she could. Then, wearily, strength fading again, she padded back along her own trail to her clothes and the tin of *teopatli*. Changing back to human form brought all her previous exhaustion and then some crashing down; she could barely persuade herself to get dressed. The only thing that moved her was the knowledge that sixteen frightened migrants waited in the darkness, knowing only what they heard: motorcycles and guns, coyotes and the roar of a jaguar. She hoped they hadn't run.

They hadn't. In desert territory none of them knew at all, it would have been suicide. Miguel stood up as Inés approached, and a few others followed suit, including the mother Inés had failed to protect from El Rojo.

The silence stretched out. She hadn't thought this far ahead, to what she would tell the migrants. Lack of energy made her blunt. "They're dead. The coyotes."

One of the other women whimpered. Inés stood, only half-listening, as a babble of questions and fear broke out. She didn't come out of her daze until Miguel drew close and said, "Do you know where we were going?"

The Tohono O'odham reservation, probably, where El Rojo would have had some means for them to continue onward. Inés didn't know what that would have been. But she knew some of the Indians protected migrants, and sent them along to others who could help.

Miguel saw it in her eyes. "You'll have to lead us, then."

Inés opened her mouth to answer him, then stopped. She had climbed the fence with these people; she had paid a coyote and gone into the desert, just like the rest of them, and that made them kin. Here in the middle of the wilderness, she could not say to Miguel, *I'm an agent of the U.S. Border Patrol. I don't do* coyotaje. *I arrest those who do.*

She would take them to the reservation, of course; it was that, or abandon them here to die. But when they arrived, she would have to hand them over, to be deported back to Mexico. Her gaze fell on the young mother, with her infant daughter. Eduardo had been the same age when their mother carried him across the border. He was eleven when they deported him, with no memory of the "home" they were sending him back to; Mamá, caught in the same raid, had gone with him. Inés, born in the United States, had stayed, and lost her family for years.

She'd joined the patrol to fight drug smuggling, to end violence, not to hunt people who only wanted work and a better life. Sneaking across the desert, risking death every step of the way, was no kind of answer—but they had no other. And Inés could not tell these frightened, hopeful men and women and children that the dream was not for them.

"We'll rest for an hour," she said. "Then I'll take you someplace safe."

SELECTION

THE APPLICATION FORM is seventy-two pages long, and they require nine copies. These people want to know *everything*. They also want to make sure you aren't doing this as a joke.

The first few pages are fairly routine. Name, date of birth, Social Security number or local equivalent—yes, you have to give them that. They promise not to use it to invade your privacy, and you trust them, because really, if they wanted to get into your bank account they could, and why would they steal *your* identity? Then education, medical history, criminal record if any—it won't necessarily disqualify you—not just for yourself, but for your family, too, *and* your close friends. (You list more distant family and friends on page seven; they'll check into those people themselves, if they decide your application is worth considering.)

Then it gets more complicated. The section people complain about the most is pages thirty-two through forty-eight: seventeen pages of moral conundrums that would have a Jesuit sweating bullets. You type up your answers to those on separate sheets. The funny thing is, it doesn't seem like they're looking for the *right* answer. They just want to know how *you* would answer. So it's best to answer honestly.

That's what people think, anyway. Nobody's really sure. Everybody tries to game the system, but very few succeed.

Maybe one in a hundred gets an interview. There are websites where people who didn't get in collate information on the interviewers; after all, you can apply again, though after a while they probably just toss your form in the trash without reading it. Who knows how good the information is, though. After all, these are the failures. The people who get in don't post about it. If you've just achieved membership in the most elite and exclusive group in the world, why would you help anyone else do the same?

If you get an interview, they'll schedule it for some evening and tell you how to get there. This is the office stage. A nice office; there's no reason any of them should put up with some flimsy room in a cubicle farm. Your interviewer may be male, female, any race, any height, any age—up to a point. They don't seem to take the really old, though there have been exceptions. They also seem not to be overweight, though maybe they lose weight after they join; there's always urban legends floating around about someone fat who got in. New members tend to go away after they join, though—off to enjoy the fruits of their effort—so it's hard to say.

The interviewer will talk to you for about two hours (sometimes more, sometimes less), then settle you down in another room for a battery of standardized tests. Mathematics, analytical reasoning, language skills, memory, hand-eye coordination; the list goes on, and not everybody gets the same tests. This usually takes until about dawn, with very few breaks.

Then you go home, and you wait to hear back.

There's no set answer for how long it will take before they notify you of your results. Could be anything from a day to a year or more. It's worse than waiting to find out if you have cancer, or so the cancer-patient applicants say.

Most people, of course, get rejected. There are billions of people on this planet; nobody knows how many apply (well, *they* do, but they're not telling), but it's a lot. Nobody knows how many of them there are, either (again, except for them), but it's not very many. Probably less than a thousandth of a percent of applicants get in. Probably a *lot* less. If one in a hundred gets that first interview, then there's a lot more winnowing down to do.

After that, the tests get weirder. They don't even tell you what half of them are, or when they're going to happen. You hit a deer on the highway, and only when you get the polite letter informing you that your application has been rejected do you find out that your behavior then was part of the test. And what did you do wrong? Were your driving skills insufficient, because you hit the deer? Should you not have stopped and gone back to see if it was alive? Are you too compassionate, too cruel, too slow, should you have *eaten* the deer?

Maybe it's all just mind-games. Maybe that's the point.

But a few, a very minuscule few, do everything right.

Those are the ones who get a second interview.

One of the most common responses to the application—all seventy-two pages of it, Jesuit-confounding moral dilemmas and all—is that there's a question missing.

They don't ask you *why*.

People go into it expecting something like a college application. (Those who have applied to college. Some people never do, and despite half-hearted attempts to prevent minors from trying for this, there *are* teenaged applicants. Even some child ones, though few of them manage the whole application. These people sometimes take minors.) You expect to be asked why you're applying. Why you want to join. Why you want to be one of this elite.

There are two reasons why they don't.

The first, and most obvious, is that the question answers itself. Why do you want to be one of the elite? Because they *are* the elite. They have power, resources, and gifts normal people can only dream of. Who *wouldn't* want to be included in their number?

The second, which most people don't ever realize, is that they don't *care*. Not to begin with, anyway.

First they'll decide whether *they* want *you*.

Few of the people who make it to the second interview say anything about it if they fail. To have made it so far, to have come so close—who wants to relive the demise of their hopes? But some details are known. There are only maybe half a dozen individuals who do these interviews, and they don't sit in offices (even nice ones) with testing equipment in the next room. They send sleek cars around—not always black, though that's the stereo-type—and bring the applicants to sumptuous houses, where silent waiters serve the guests seven-course meals with hummingbird tongues in honey-glaze sauce. If you've made it this far, then they think they might want you, and though it isn't remotely necessary for them to demonstrate their wealth and power—you know about it, or you wouldn't have applied—they like to show off a bit.

This is when they ask you why.

Again, as with all of the tests, who knows if there's even a correct answer? Maybe what they're really looking for is variety, and if you sound too much like everyone else, then you're out. Maybe they want you to entertain them with your response. Maybe they're judging you based on whether or not you set your fork down while you answer, and if so, whether you put it on the plate or on the table.

Nobody knows their logic, or whether they even have any.

So you answer. You can't avoid the question. And you probably thought about it when you picked up the application, before you knew the "why" question wasn't on there. Maybe your answers have changed since then; maybe they haven't. Med students say it's like being asked why you want to be a doctor, only much, much more stressful. Certainly the answers given in med school interviews would probably not work here. If you get in, you'll be taking from those around you rather than giving back; you'll be hurting instead of healing. (Though most of those you hurt will be volunteers. They're not hard to find. Getting past their teeming hordes to something a bit more interesting is the hard part.)

They don't ask you whether you're aware of what you'll be giving up. Three reasons this time. One is that, if the rumors are true, they can get rid of you if you decide you made a mistake. Second, if you've made it this far, then you've thought about that question a million times, and answered it to your satisfaction; you *can* back out during the process, if you change your mind.

The third is that really, who cares? What you'll be giving up is nothing next to what you'll be gaining.

You finish your dinner, your host smiles at you and says they'll be in touch, and the sleek car takes you home.

Virtually all of the select few who get this far have already started training.

There's no real need, but they do it anyway. It's one of the ways you know someone around you has gotten past the early stages. (Some people don't like to talk about it, for fear of jinxing themselves.) Don't waste your time taking them to a psychiatrist; the doctor will shrug and tell you to leave it be. If your friend fails, then he'll stop on his own or you can take him to therapy then. If he succeeds, well, this will be his life. (In a manner of speaking.)

If there's still any chance of you backing out, you'll do it now. Virtually no one does.

The third interview, no one really knows anything about.

People say it's not actually an interview. They don't know if anybody fails at this point; failures, if there are any, are never seen again. They *do* know that the third interview is with one man. It has to be; he's the only one who can induct you.

Induct you. It's an odd phrase. Sounds like a fraternity ritual. It isn't.

No one outside the group knows who he is, or where he is, or where he goes. People taken to the third interview are picked up by a small, private plane, and no government or other organization in the world is stupid enough to try and track that craft. It touches down, takes on its passenger, and vanishes.

If you're on that plane, then you're taken somewhere (or

maybe he's on the plane with you), and you talk to him (or maybe you don't), and you succeed (or maybe fail, and vanish for all time).

If you're on the plane, and you don't fail, then you become one of them.

One of us. I can call myself that now.

Nothing I've said in this document betrays any of our secrets. I still am not going to post it, and I imagine they would stop me if I tried. You don't join the most powerful and influential people in the world without understanding that they have ways of doing pretty much anything they want to. That power does not become yours instantaneously when you join, but it happens quickly; after all, we've already decided whether we want you and trust you. If we bring you in, then you're one of us. End of story.

Or beginning of story. The day is lost to you, but the night is your domain. You will be eternally unaging, eternally perfect. People the world over will throw themselves at your feet, begging for your touch—if you want more challenging prey, you'll have to go looking. Power and wealth will be at your fingertips; you can spend a century perfecting your knowledge of physics or Spanish poetry or military techniques of the ancient world. Eternity is yours. Do with it what you like.

Just don't whine about it. They get rid of the angsty ones quickly, quietly, and without a fuss.

SUCH AS DREAMS
ARE MADE OF

HOLT CLOSED HIS CELLPHONE, the soft click swallowed up by the cool grey carpet, and smiled to himself. His next deal was well underway, even as he stood in the monument of his latest achievement. The room that would become his office was empty still, the furniture not yet delivered, but he wasn't unduly impatient. Corner-cutting and well-placed bribes had finished this office tower ahead of schedule and under budget. After years of this work, Holt was a master of his art.

He enjoyed the challenge of it, more than the result. Construction could be interesting, but the true sport was in the negotiations, buying out properties for redevelopment. The craft market that had once stood here was the hardest battle he'd fought yet, pitting him against a neighborhood association that wanted to save the old two-story building with its gaudy mural walls from the forces of modern urban planning. A year and a half, before he won that one. But now the craft market was only a memory, and ultimately even less than that. That was why he'd chosen to move his office here. There were few things more satisfying than staking out territory in a conquered land.

Holt smiled to himself and straightened his suit, taking one last look around before turning off the light and exiting into the hall.

He pulled up short as a man almost ran into him. "Watch where you're—" Holt began.

He never got to the last word before a fist crashed into his head.

"See for yourself." The cop gestured for Holt to watch the clip.

Scowling, Holt dragged his flimsy chair forward until it was right in front of the TV. He *would* see for himself. If this cop was too incompetent to do his job, Holt would do it for him.

He blessed the luck that had gotten the building's security cameras installed just two days before. No one had seen the thug who attacked him exiting the building; at that late hour, not many people were around. The eye of technology, though, was always watching.

The empty hallway flickered up onto the screen. Holt focused on it, glancing at all the corners of the image, looking for a tell-tale shadow that might give away the bastard's hiding place.

He saw no shadows. But after a few seconds of the unchanging image, he saw the door to his office open, saw himself step into the hall. His image scowled and mouthed a few words.

Then he staggered backward, hit the wall, and slid down it to land in a crumpled heap on the floor.

And through it all, there was no one else in the hall.

The cop rewound the tape without being asked. Holt watched it again, lips pressed together. He saw himself fall at no visible hand. He could not tear his eyes away from the sight of his body lying on the floor, a heap of expensively tailored suit and un-responsive flesh.

"You see why we're confused," the cop said. "You claim to have been attacked by a man you ran into in the hall. But there's nobody on the tape. Unless he's invisible?"

Holt glared at him. "I doubt that," he said icily. "There were a number of people who opposed my buyout of that property. Perhaps one of them doctored the tape."

"We'll look into it," the cop said, but his voice reeked of skepticism.

"Do you think I'm lying?" Holt demanded. "I didn't hit *myself* in the head. And I'm not faking this. Ask the doctor who treated me."

"We did." The cop flipped his folder open and scanned a sheet of paper inside. "The doctor found no contusion on your head. No bruise."

"I know what a contusion is," Holt snapped.

The cop continued without batting an eyelash at the outburst. "He says here that maybe your experience took place inside your own brain. A chemical imbalance, which made you hallucinate and then black out."

Holt slapped his hand down onto the table. "I do not use drugs. My blood tests will prove that."

"We're not accusing you of anything. The problem could be natural."

The words took a moment to sink in. When they did, Holt's blood turned to ice. "A tumor?"

"You'll have to discuss that with the doctor." The cop stood. "Call us if you remember anything else that might be of use. Or if anything else happens."

"Like another attack."

"Yes." The cop's eyes gave nothing away. He would have made a good businessman.

When the cop was gone, Holt sat back and closed his eyes. His blood had not yet warmed up again, leaving him cold all through.

That man *hadn't* been a hallucination. He'd been too vivid, too immediately there. Granted, the fellow had looked peculiar, with his bright clothing all shredded and stained, hanging in rags off his bony frame, but if Holt had been seeing things, why had he imagined a man? Why not something stranger?

Holt thought of the man's furious presence, and retracted that thought. He *had* been stranger. And frightening, too, his eyes reflecting the light until they seemed to glow.

A tumor, or else simple madness.

Holt wasn't sure which possibility scared him more.

❖

Work. That was what he needed. Work would distract him from the empty hallway, from the appointment for a CAT scan in three days' time. He spent most of the next day in his office, piling work on his secretary until she was too busy to make timid suggestions that he go home and rest. He didn't need rest; he needed distraction.

He needed reassurance, confirmation that his world was still under his control. Holt got in his car and drove across the city, to look over the site of his next triumph.

The theatre's walls rose around him, claustrophobically close. The place seated barely three hundred. Holt walked down the aisle, looking from side to side at the old seats with their carved wooden frames and worn velvet cushions. They would be sold off before the building was demolished. He couldn't imagine who would want one. The velvet bred dust, and probably harbored insects.

He arrived at the stage and stopped there, looking up at the heavy curtain of crimson velvet, bordered by ugly carvings covered in flaking gilt paint. They looked like termites had been chewing on them. This place would probably fall down on its own in another ten years, even without his help.

"Please—do not do it."

Holt spun, immediately on the defensive. But the speaker wasn't the man who had attacked him; it was a woman. A tiny thing, almost child-like, clothed in some kind of antique brocade dress that matched the theatre's decor. An actress, he supposed. The tension went out of his muscles. Were they putting on one last play, before the building fell?

"I suppose your fellow actors sent you to plead with me," Holt said, straightening. She would barely come up to his collarbone, if she stood next to him.

She shook her head. Curls tumbled around her shoulders with the motion. Whoever had nominated her as their spokeswoman obviously didn't know Holt. He believed in reasoned arguments and money, not big-eyed waifs. "I was not sent," she said.

Holt shrugged. "Doesn't matter. Whatever you have to say, I

don't want to hear it."

He moved to pass her and leave the building, but she stood in his way. "Please," she repeated. "Why do you need to destroy this playhouse? There are other places you could build."

"There are other places you could perform," Holt countered. "The new Arts Center seats two thousand."

"It's huge," the woman said, as if the adjective tasted bad. "No intimacy."

"But much more revenue." Why was he even wasting his time talking to her? Why hadn't he left already? She couldn't stop him.

Holt realized with a sudden chill that he didn't want to go near her, as he would have to in order to continue up the aisle. He could cross to a different aisle, but that would make him look scared. And he refused to run from a woman half his size, no matter how unnerving her eyes were.

He steeled himself and shoved past her.

He was almost to the lobby when she spoke again. "He should not have attacked you."

Holt whirled. She still stood in the aisle, hands folded neatly across her brocaded skirt. He stared at her, grasping for words, and finally growled, "Tell him to stay away from me. *Far* away." He would tell the police to follow her. She might lead them to the man.

"For what he did, you have my apology," she said. "I told him it would do no good."

"It'll get him in jail," Holt snarled.

She shook her head. "No. But he cares not for reason; his tragedy has left him insensible to all but rage." Her eyes were sad, but she stared unwaveringly at Holt, and he refused to look away. He wouldn't let her cow him. "Many are angry. Some agree with him, and say that to do a great right we must do a little wrong."

Fury made Holt tremble. "Don't threaten me, bitch. I'll see you locked up. All of you. The police are onto your friend, and you can bet I'll tell them about you, too."

She did not look frightened, or even taken aback. Just sad. And now, a touch amused as well. "What will you tell them?" she asked. "That you were threatened by a ghost?"

Then she vanished.

When the call came, Holt almost refused. But the theatre manager was adamant: if his building was going to be torn down, he was going to spend as much of his remaining time there as he could. The meeting had to be in *his* office.

Holt didn't want to go, didn't want to set foot anywhere near that building. Not since the CAT scan had come back clean. There was nothing wrong with his brain—nothing that could explain what he had seen.

Which left only the possibility that he was going mad.

And if anyone else found out about it...the field he worked in was cutthroat. The slightest hint of weakness, the merest doubt as to his competence, and his career would be over. Hallucinations might as well be a death sentence.

But the manager insisted, until Holt grew disgusted with his own timidity. What could a wisp like that woman do to him? She was probably the ghost of some actress who had died on stage. She probably couldn't even leave the hall. The building's offices weren't her kind of territory.

She wasn't even *real*.

So Holt went.

The manager wanted to show him a petition, of all things. A bunch of signatures under a little paragraph of quasi-legal babble asking him to leave the theatre standing. Holt scanned it and tossed it back onto the desk. "Names don't move me, Mr. Wharton."

The manager's face was white and strained. "There are over—"

"I don't care how many there are. This is valuable property, and it could be much more productively developed. The owner agrees."

"Because you offered him ten times as much money." Red was creeping up Wharton's neck to his face.

Holt smiled. This was familiar territory. "Exactly. Meet my offer, and then we might have something to talk about."

"You know we can't."

"Yes." Holt's smile widened.

The manager glared at him. "This isn't over, Mr. Holt. This building is nearly a hundred years old; it's quite an important place. We're working to get it classified as a historical landmark."

Ah. Holt had been wondering if the man would think of this particular tactic. "I wish you luck, Mr. Wharton, but such designations take a terribly long time to go through." He'd have the deal closed long before then, and the building reduced to so much historical rubble.

"We're appealing to a judge to have the deal postponed."

Interesting. Holt might actually have to do something about this. It all depended on who the judge was. There were a few who owed him favors. "You're welcome to try."

Wharton stood. "Wait here, Mr. Holt. I want to show you something."

Holt didn't bother to hide his impatience. "Be quick. I dislike wasting my time."

The manager growled as if he wanted to respond to that but could find no decent answer. Once the man left the office, Holt smiled again. He loved a good fight.

"He wasn't always like that, you know."

Holt leapt out of his chair. She was there, without warning, without coming through the goddamned door. She sat—no, *perched* on the edge of a row of filing cabinets. Her antique dress ought to have been terribly out of place among the steel furniture and computers. But her presence forced Holt's awareness beyond those trappings to what lay behind: the office, its walls and floor and ceiling, with old wooden beams and whitewashed plaster in between, all a part of the same building that housed the stage. Nearly a hundred years old. She fit in just fine. It was the modern material that didn't belong. And try though he might to deny her reality, his efforts disintegrated when faced with her presence.

"Not the manager," she continued, unfazed by Holt's violent movement. "The other. We change, you see, as the buildings do. And if they are destroyed too soon—" Her eyes were grim, and sad. "That way madness lies."

Holt tugged his suit straight and pulled himself together. "And why should I care?"

She looked at him with her disquieting eyes. "You have come within the measure of our wrath."

"You can't do anything to me," Holt said, putting more confidence behind it than he felt. "You're dead."

A smile flickered across her doll-like face. "I am not dead."

He stared at her. A terrible suspicion welled up in him, that he'd been played for a fool. "You said you were a ghost."

She looked apologetic. "I...misspoke. For the sake of rhetorical force. It's a failing many theatre people have."

Holt was hardly listening. Not a ghost. In which case—

He lunged forward and seized her wrist. His fingers closed around birdlike bones and soft skin. She looked amused, and for a moment he wanted to fling her into a wall, just to wipe the look off her face.

He settled for dragging her toward the office door. Whatever smoke-and-mirrors trick she and her friends had pulled the other day, she'd have trouble managing it with him holding onto her.

Which was a fine plan as far as it went, but then her wrist melted out of his grasp.

She didn't pull free. She didn't break his hold. She simply wasn't there anymore. Holt's fingers suddenly came together, with nothing inside. He turned and found her standing behind him. She gave a little shrug that might have been an apology.

"Not a ghost," she said. "But I never said I was human."

He turned to bolt for the door and there she was, blocking his way. She hadn't walked there. She stared at him with her unnatural eyes, and for a moment he saw lightning flicker in them, deep inside. Not human at all.

"Will you not leave my playhouse alone?" she asked.

Holt staggered back until he hit his chair.

She glided toward him, delicate and terrifying, a symptom of his madness—and yet she felt so *real*—

Holt took refuge in what he knew: stubbornness. "No."

She was close now, and her tiny size belied the presence that filled the whole room—the whole *building*. "This is my place," she said, speaking with clear, cold enunciation, and he believed it. "I will not let you destroy it."

The door behind her opened, and she vanished.

Holt shoved past Wharton without a word, ignoring the papers the man tried to put into his hand. He had to get out of the building. Had to get away from her, back to where things made sense. Back to reality.

He managed to walk to the outside door. A fast walk, but a walk. Then, once outside, Holt ran for his car.

He slept—if it could be called sleep. He drifted in and out, never quite awake, never quite asleep, despite the pills he'd taken. When he was alert enough to know he was awake, he was angry. He had let an incorporeal slip of a woman—not even a woman!—put him to flight. A mere fancy of the imagination. She couldn't possibly exist. The stress of his job had cracked him at last, and he had gone mad.

But he couldn't make himself believe it. He *wasn't* imagining her.

That thought, which sat so uncomfortably in his mind, brought him awake.

Thunder was rumbling uneasily outside, disturbing his attempts at sleep. Holt's tossing and turning had left most of the sheets hanging off the sides of the bed. He sat up to retrieve them—and saw it.

The street lamp outside cast just enough light to reveal the figure standing at the foot of the bed. Holt opened his mouth to order the intruder out, but no words came. A presence filled the room, making the very walls pulse. A cold presence, possessed of an unblinking regard that pinned Holt to his bed like a moth on a card. The figure was thin to the point of emaciation, stick-like, mere bones wrapped in skin. It was roughly human, but consisted of angles and lengths that were not quite right. In size it was neither child nor adult, and it showed no hint of gender.

Holt didn't have to be told that it was another one of them. The way his skin was crawling made that quite plain.

But he was damned if he'd let them intimidate him here. This was *his* place; they had no right to intrude on him. Holt cleared his throat and glared at the figure. "Get out," he said. Just that, nothing more. His brain tried to formulate a tirade, but inspiration withered and died under the thing's stare.

Part of him still insisted the creature could not be there. The apartment building was full of wealthy young professionals, mostly unmarried; there were no children. No one so silly and irrational as to believe in a creature like this. How could it possibly live here, in such an atmosphere?

It didn't live here. It *was* here. This place.

Just as she was the playhouse…

…and the other one was—had been—the craft market.

Holt could not tear his eyes away from the thing at the end of his bed. It stood, watching him, and he wondered if it too would attack him. And if so, how he could possibly defend himself.

Lightning flashed, bleaching the room bone-white and forcing Holt's eyes shut. When he opened them, the spirit was gone.

The theatre's front door was unlocked, even though it was the middle of the night. He found her inside, standing on the stage. The heavy curtains had been drawn back, and a single light shone down on her, making the curls of her hair into a golden halo. Holt stood in the aisle, dripping rainwater onto the threadbare carpet, and glared at her.

"That *thing*. Did you send it after me?"

She shook her head. "It was always there. Once you were blind, but now you see. Did it bother you?" Her voice carried a mocking edge. "You made it, you realize."

"I—"

She stopped Holt's denial before he could form it. "All of you, who live in that place. Frozen and harsh. But not soulless, no—only a very new building lacks a spirit. But the one you made for that place is twisted. Unhappy. Like you."

"I'm perfectly happy."

"You are cold. Heartless. Without love. Some who live there are different, but many are like you, and together you made what you saw." Holt saw pity in her eyes, but it was not for him. She grieved for that monster, the one she said he had made.

"Don't go blaming me for that thing," he growled. "I never asked for any of you to exist."

"You don't *get* to ask," she said. The advantage of height the stage had given her made her tiny body imposing. All around him he could feel the theatre's walls, strong despite their age and worn appearance, strong with her power. They would not fail until she did, and she showed no sign of weakness. "Do you think you could live, work, *dream*, and it would have no effect?" She spread her arms wide, as if taking the entire theatre into her embrace. "We are such stuff as dreams are made of. From the elderly man who funded the raising of this playhouse out of his private fortune and his love of theatre, to the boy who sweeps the stage after the curtain has fallen and everyone has gone home, who looks out at the empty seats and dreams of glory and art—they have made me, all unknowing. That boy weeps for me, and for himself, because he thinks that I must leave him."

"Yes, and it's all my fault," Holt said nastily. "All of it, from that creature in my room to your untimely demise. You're this building? This building is a hundred years old. You're out of date, bitch. The world has moved on, and it's left you behind."

"As it left *him* behind?" She turned and began to walk across the front of the stage, casual as an actress giving a soliloquy. "You should have seen him, when the craft market still stood. He would caper about like a jester, giving flowers to ladies and sweets to children. He made them laugh."

"How do I stop seeing you?" Holt demanded. "How do I make you leave me alone?"

She turned, a slow pivot that brought her around until she faced him squarely. "Leave *us* alone."

Holt snorted. "I have a living to make. And I'm good at what I do."

"Indeed, you are Covetousness incarnate. You wish to turn this playhouse into gold, that you might lock it up in your chest." Her voice carried a razor-sharp edge of bitterness. "You craft most foul and unnatural murder."

Murdering her was sounding more pleasant by the second. "I'm looking forward to closing you down. I'll come watch the demolition, just to be sure you're really gone." Would it send her mad, as it had the other one? Holt found himself hoping it would. Anger gave him courage. He didn't fear her. He didn't fear *any* of them.

As if she could read his mind, a smile ghosted across her painted lips. "Of course you should not fear us. We are but daggers of the mind, false creations, begot of nothing but vain fantasy. What can such as we do to you?"

Her words only confirmed Holt's own thoughts, but something in them, a mocking tone almost too faint to hear, choked off his growing feeling of confidence. He stared at her, and she smiled back.

He whirled, but there was no one else in the room. No one sneaking up on him. Then why was she smiling? "They will not come here," she said. "No one will. We are bound to our places."

But she spoke of the others as if she knew them. "You talk to each other," he said, looking at her.

Her smile grew a whimsical twist. "How else are we to pass the quiet hours, when we stand empty and alone?"

They talked to each other. And she was smiling as if she knew something he didn't.

"We have a speech of fire that fain would blaze," she said. The humor had leached out of her voice, leaving her grim and cold, and the lightning was in her eyes. "You will hear it anon."

Holt spun and ran for the exit.

She was standing there, in front of the door to the lobby, but he charged up the aisle toward her anyway. Corporeal or not, he would get past her. He had to get out of here.

"The bright day is done," she said as he approached. "We are for the dark, and may do such bitter business as the day would quake to look on."

A heartbeat before he would have crashed into her, she vanished.

He felt eyes on him as he drove through the streets, as if the buildings were watching him. Holt felt the force of all the spirits, all the personalities accumulated by years of habitation and dreaming. He drove faster and faster through the nighttime streets, slick with rain, and tried to ignore them all.

Despite his speed, the fire trucks beat him there.

The office building was doomed by the time Holt arrived. Three fire trucks were lined up outside, and a fourth screeched in as he pulled to a stop, but their sprays had hardly any effect. Nearly all twenty stories were on fire; they wouldn't be able to salvage much. Years of work were going up in smoke.

An ambulance was parked off to the left. Paramedics stood around it, idle as the firemen were not. This was not an apartment building; there was no one to rescue. A police officer was with them. Holt headed for him.

"What happened?" he shouted as he came close.

The cop glanced at him. "Are you the owner of this building?"

"I oversaw its construction."

"Your name, sir?"

"Holt. What happened to the building?"

A gurney rolled past as he asked the question. Holt's eyes shot to it, but the occupant was covered in a sheet from head to toe.

"Who's that?" he demanded.

"A homeless man appears to have been sleeping in the building when it went up," the cop said.

Fury brought blood surging up into Holt's face. So this was their revenge. The spirit of the craft market had set fire to the office building. Lucky for him he'd died in the flames; Holt would have killed him, otherwise. "Arson," he snarled.

"Doesn't look like it, Mr. Holt," the cop said. "We think it's an electrical fire. There'll be an investigation, of course, once the flames have died down, but that seems the most likely cause." He flipped a notebook open and fished a pen out of his pocket. "You say you were involved with the building's construction? I'll need your address and phone number, and the name of the contractor you hired for the wiring."

Holt smiled through gritted teeth. This wasn't anything he couldn't handle. Easy enough to place the blame on the electrical contractor, as if he hadn't known all along that the man was cutting corners. A bit of suspicion would attach to Holt, but that was fine. They hadn't stopped him.

Holt took the cop's notebook and wrote down his contact information. The building was a loss, yes, but he would come out of the situation all right.

And then he'd go after that bitch and her "playhouse."

He came home in the chill hours before dawn, more than ready to sleep. Another storm was rolling in, but no amount of thunder could keep him awake at this point. The adrenaline had long since worn off, leaving him cold and tired.

Holt let himself into the apartment, hung up his coat, and walked into the living room.

It was waiting for him.

The sticklike figure stood just a pace or two away. Its dead eyes held fragments of the lightning that split the sky outside. Holt had a vision of leaping forward, taking that brittle body in his hands and breaking it until it could no longer stand and look at him with those horrible eyes.

He had the vision, but he could not do it.

Who was to say this building could not suffer its own "electrical fire"? With him in it?

The thing in front of him raised its hand, and to his bone-deep shame Holt flinched as if struck. But the creature did not move toward him.

There was something in its hand.

Papers.

Holt recognized them. Files, taken from the desk in his apartment office. The letterhead on the front one was identifiable even in the unpredictable illumination of the lightning. It was a proposal for an upcoming projects.

The papers burst into flame.

The thing holding them did not flinch even as embers began to float free, drifting down to scorch its hand and arm. It held the burning sheaf there, in front of Holt, keeping his eyes riveted to the destruction.

Files. Just files. But the message was clear.

Anything he built, they would destroy. Maybe not electrical fires every time; maybe the windows would loosen and fall, or the foundation would crack. Different flaws, but adding up. Everything he did from now on, they would know about, and there would be nothing he could do to guard himself against them. One "accident" he could handle without losing his career, but not a dozen.

They wouldn't kill him. They would just ruin him. Completely.

Holt did move then, and screamed, and threw himself at the creature standing before him. But it was gone the moment he moved, and he fell to his knees in the cinders, left alone amidst the ashes of his future.

La Molejera

I HEAR THE SOUND well before I reach the end of the path, an awful, rocky, percussive scraping that makes my teeth hurt. They say she's at it all day, every day; if it weren't for the charity of the village, the old woman would have starved long ago. She's not grinding corn in that metate of hers, and she won't be making any tortillas from the meal.

The path to her hut on the hill is overgrown and treacherous, and I keep an eye out for snakes. Hardly anyone comes this way, except the feather-boy, and his trips to bring her food aren't enough to make much of an impression on the lianas and ferns that threaten to choke the way off completely. I make my way through an oppressive green tunnel, sweating my bug spray off already even though it's barely ten a.m., and there's a corner of my mind wondering if I can make use of this moment when I write my ethnography. Wretched experiences, adding color to anthropological writing, for the use of. It helps me be philosophical about the mosquitos.

The tunnel of green finally opens up, and I emerge into a blaze of sunlight that makes my eyes water. I think at first that the movement I see is just from the tears, but as my vision steadies, I see snakes slithering off into the undergrowth. Fer-de-lances. I carefully swallow my heart, which has migrated up to my mouth. Why would a woman who's terrified of snakes choose to do research in a snake-infested region of Veracruz? All in the name of science, I suppose.

The old woman does not look up as I try to convince myself it's safe to move. Her wrinkled, bony hands grip the grinding stone, the mano, driving it forward, back, forward, back, and the awful scraping sound is even worse up close. It vibrates in the marrow of my bones. I force myself to take a step toward her, hoping that moving will help relieve the tension; it doesn't, but now I've committed myself, and have to keep going even though I want to turn and bolt back down the path.

She still doesn't look up. The villagers say she doesn't stop for anything except the feather-boy's visits, though how they know that when it seems like none of them ever come up here, I don't know. I can't even ask anyone. I'm pretty sure they don't want me visiting her.

The mano scrapes along, crushing bits of stone beneath it. Looks like limestone to me, pale against the darker basalt of the metate. I wonder if there's any way for me to get a sample of it. Where does she get the stone, anyway? Does the feather-boy bring it to her? And what does she do with all the powder she creates?

I can't ask the people of the village, and I can't ask her, either. I open my mouth to do it, to say hello, introduce myself, get a conversation going that will allow me to work around to the thousand questions I have, and nothing comes out. The woman grinds away, stone on stone, ignoring me as if I weren't there. I've found La Molejera, and now I don't know what to do with myself.

After an eternity of awkward silence, I mouth an apology I can't quite voice and back away down the trail, wondering how big a mistake I've just made.

Cultural Research Foundation Grant Proposal
Anita Muñoz, University of California at Los Angeles

Indigenous Religious Practices Among the Nahua Indians of Veracruz

...the technological changes brought to the Huasteca region of

Veracruz, as driven by a variety of government initiatives, in combination with social changes such as the recent influx of Protestant missionaries, have combined to decrease observance of the older costumbre *religion (the "religion of customs"). In many Nahua villages, no new individuals have been trained as shamans, so that the current elderly generation of practitioners will be the last…*

…although many of the benefits the Nahuas (or Macehualli, as they prefer to be called) were formerly able to derive from their social position as Indians have faded in recent years, at least one small region of the Huasteca still maintains the indigenous religion to a remarkably high degree…

…the purpose of my project is to conduct anthropological research in the village of Chalchihuitlan and examine the question of why the indigenous religion is maintained there, when other villages have decreased their practice of it or abandoned it entirely. What combination of factors makes its perpetuation in Chalchihuitlan a productive social, political, or economic strategy for the Macehualli of that area?…

I couched it in suitably academic language when I wrote my grant proposal, but the truth is I went there because of my abuela. Because of her stories. My clearest memories of childhood involve sitting on our back porch, listening to her talk while her old, wrinkled hands ground corn in her metate. Mamá used to nag her about that, in the half-hearted way you do when the argument's been going on for decades and you know you're not going to win. *You don't have to grind that by hand, you know; we could get you a machine, or you could just buy tortillas ready-made…* Then Rosa would give her daughter a dirty look for having the temerity to suggest she not make her own tortillas.

I burned every tortilla I ever made, but I learned the stories. And then I traced them back to their source, to the village where she was born. Chalchihuitlan, "the place of jade," a place which hardly seemed to have changed one bit in all the years since my abuela left. When villages all over the Huasteca were giving up on their old rituals and beliefs, the people of her home were different. And I wanted to know why.

Coming here was the strangest experience of my life. I'd been communicating with the village's municipal agent don Alejandro for nearly a year by the time I showed up, arranging everything necessary for my fieldwork, but that had been by mail, messenger, and a single international phone call. Before I started my dissertation fieldwork, I hadn't set foot in Chalchihuitlan (or Chalchi, as I called it in the privacy of my head, where only the memory of my abuela could glare at me for chopping it short). I showed up expecting to be a stranger, and in most ways I was— more mexicana than india, more chicana than mexicana. But I was *their* stranger.

Don Alejandro's wife Magdalena took me around Chalchi like I was some kind of exotic animal on parade, introducing me to one woman after another while the men were out working in the milpas, planting and tending the corn. At every house, we went through the dance again, explaining who I was, establishing me in the intricate web of relationships that makes up Chalchi. Anita Muñoz the anthropologist was a poor second to the grand-daughter of Rosa Martínez, among these people. *María Elena's grandfather Pedro,* doña Magdalena would say, *you remember, who lived at the bend in the arroyo, he had a coyotl compadre in Tuxpan—* Compadre, not a simple friend as the dictionary would translate it, but a ritual relative, and a corner of my mind was taking notes on fictive kinship and its role in rural Macehualli life. Not the subject of my research, but you pay attention to everything in the field, as much as you can, until your head overflows. *And when the man Pedro's sister Rosa was going to marry died, his compadre gave her a job in Santa Angelina so she could earn some money, and would you believe it, they fell in love and got married.* And then the *really* strange part of the story, about how one of Rosa's daughters married another coyotl— around me, people mostly avoided calling him a mestizo, the

offensive name for a non-Indian—and they emigrated to the
States, to Texas, and when Rosa was widowed she went to live
with her daughter. Her daughter, not her youngest son, the way
it would be done here. But Rosa had no sons.

At every house, I smiled nervously and said hello, excruciatingly
aware, for the first time in my life, of how I spoke Spanish like an
American, and how I spoke Nahuatl like a fumble-tongued grad
student. And they smiled back and didn't comment on it, because
they are more polite than that. Research was getting off to a
swimming start.

Then I stepped on my first fieldwork land mine, in the form
of seven-year-old Pepe Rodríguez.

He was helping his mother hang laundry when we showed up,
me tagging along at doña Magdalena's heels like one of the dogs
that wander all around the village. Small talk lasts forever among
these people, endless rounds of commentary on casual subjects
before we get to anything of substance, but we were only a little
way into it when Pepe's mother ushered him forward and said
with obvious pride, "This is my son. He's the feather-boy."

I mis-stepped. I'd read books on the Macehualli, and I'd dealt
with my abuela, but she'd lost many of her native ways and books
don't prepare you for real live people. I forgot to be indirect, I
forgot to respect the pace of the conversation, and I jumped on
that word like a starving anthropologist. "Feather-boy? What's
that? Is it some kind of ritual position?"

The boy's mother smiled in a way I remembered my abuela
doing when the situation turned awkward. "Go ask the shaman."

(excerpt from Chalchihuitlan field notes, undated)

Idiom translation guide:
"What does your heart say?" = *How are you?*
"To put down flowers" = *to hold a ritual*
"Go ask the shaman" = *I'm not going to tell you, so please
stop asking questions*

I had my choice of shamans to ask; that was one of the things that made this place so unusual. But just because Chalchi boasted more than half a dozen shamans didn't mean I could just stroll up and start asking them things. They were very good at gently dodging questions they didn't want to answer. Which made me impatient, so I pressed harder, and then they shut down more, because I was being pushy and aggressive like a mestiza, or worse, a gringa. They were half-willing to accept me because of my abuela, but not when I acted like this. I had to slow down, learn to be indirect, and chew on the trees in frustration only when I was alone.

It paid off. María Francisca, a seventy-two-year-old shaman who got around in the forest as nimbly as a monkey while I blundered heavily in her wake, finally let me come to a curing ritual. I kept my mouth shut and watched as she burned copal and waved brushes of leaves and chanted and tore up paper images of the wind spirits causing the illness, and then afterward we talked. And this time, I was indirect. In fact, I wasn't even thinking about the feather-boy. That, I was rapidly learning, was the way of fieldwork: you get your most useful information when you're not looking for it.

"She's very young," María Francisca was saying of her helper, eleven-year-old Catalina. "Some say too young. But it takes a long time to learn to be a shaman, to teach someone, and I'm old. I don't have much time left." She cackled cheerfully, sounding not at all old.

"Has she been helping you long?" I asked.

"Less than a year. But she's always helped in the rituals, the way a lot of the children do. Like in the winter, when we bring *tonantsij* out. You missed that one, but we'll show you next time. The children help in other ways, too. They gather things for us that we need in our rituals, or little Pepe Rodríguez, the feather-boy, he takes food to La Molejera."

I almost swallowed my tongue.

Instead I swallowed the eight thousand questions that tried to leap past my lips and offered a tentative statement, hoping to nudge the conversation forward. "I remember my abuela telling stories about her. That she's always grinding stone, doesn't stop for anything."

"Except the feather-boy. Yes. I'm not surprised your abuela remembered; she would not forget La Molejera."

"I thought she was an old woman, though," I said casually. "Even when my grandmother was young. She's still around?"

But my attempt at delicacy failed. The shaman's face closed up. "Oh, yes. We feed her well. But she doesn't like visitors." And the conversation ended.

(excerpt from Chalchihuitlan field notes, 6/21)

M.F. mentioned Pepe/feather-boy thing in context of RITUAL, of RELIGION. La M's some kind of religious thing? Abuela said she was old DECADES ago. How can she still be alive? World's oldest woman? Or always a La M, and they replace her when old one dies?

I have to assume people know I've gone to seen La Molejera. Or do they? If no one visits her except the feather-boy, little Pepe, then they'll only know if she's told Pepe, and if he's told someone else. Or if they saw me climbing the narrow path up her hill. But I don't think they know, because no one's said anything to me.

So of course I go back.

The green tunnel closes in on me again and I wonder why I'm doing this. Is it good fieldwork? Not when they've made it clear they don't want me prying into this old woman's life. I can't leave it alone, though. When I go to sleep, I hear her grinding stone, as if she keeps going all night, as if I can hear her through the thick forest that separates us.

I doubt going back will fix that, but I brave the snakes and go anyway.

She's in her usual place, hard at work. The Grinding One:

that's what "La Molejera" means. Don't need to be a brilliant anthropologist to figure out where the name came from.

I wait for a while, as Macehualli often do when they arrive at someone's house, because they don't want to interrupt. She still doesn't look up, and I can't quite bring myself, in the face of her absolute disregard for my presence, to launch into the usual spiel about my great-uncle Pedro's mestizo compadre. But at least this time I find my voice.

"Good morning, grandmother," I say to her respectfully. It comes out in Nahuatl without me even thinking about it, and not because I'm afraid this woman doesn't speak Spanish. Most of the people of Chalchi know at least a little. No, I just can't imagine addressing this woman in some foreign European tongue. Her clothing is obviously hand-sewn, very traditional, covered in gorgeous but faded embroidery; she's sitting barefoot in front of a leaf-thatched house, working with mano y metate; this could be the fifteenth century and I doubt there would be any difference.

Scrape, scrape, scrape, goes the mano.

"My name is Anita Muñoz," I say after a moment, when it has become obvious she's not going to return my greeting. "I'm a visitor to Chalchihuitlan. From the United States."

She continues to work, and I clench my teeth briefly against the unpleasant sound before I manage to go on. "I don't mean to disturb your work—" What a joke. She wouldn't stop grinding for anything less than the end of the world. "But I've been introduced to most of the people in this village, and I thought it would be rude not to greet you."

There are no piles of stone nearby for her to put into her metate, and no piles of powder from it. She *must* stop once in a while, then, to get more stone to work on, and dump the stuff she's done with. But I can't go prying into her house to find it. Forget anthropological ethics; I just can't imagine doing it. Somebody else's house, maybe. Not hers.

The silence stretches out until I can't take it anymore. Just being in her presence makes my hair stand on end, even in this heat. "I apologize for interrupting you," I say. "I'll leave you alone." And she takes as little notice of that as she does of anything else.

As I turn to leave a second time, flustered by my failure, dizzied by the heat, for a moment my vision swims again, and the stone of her metate looks different. Not the darkness of basalt, but the green of jade.

Then I regain my balance, the stone goes back to normal, and I re-enter the forest tunnel, despairing of ever finding out who and what this ancient woman is.

(excerpt from Chalchihuitlan field notes, 8/7)

Collected Chicomexochitl stories today. Wasn't Chicomexochitl an Aztec god? Means "seven flower." Connected with corn.

NOTE TO SELF: Lunch with Dr. Westerfeld next week. Go to office while in Tuxpan, change out books. Left too many books in town, brought wrong ones to village.

Fieldwork is supposed to be immersive; I felt like I was cheating when I made the trek to Tuxpan and found myself suddenly back in the mestizo world. After so long in the forest, where the biggest open spaces were the milpas crowded with growing corn, Tuxpan seemed gaspingly bare of trees. All around me voices were speaking Spanish, glorious Spanish, that I didn't have to struggle to understand; their regional accents were a cakewalk compared to the thicket of Nahuatl.

My relief at leaving Chalchi for a while was like a splash of cold water, reminding me of how much I *didn't* fit in there. Some of the villagers had decided to accept me, but many still considered me nothing more than a pushy, meddling mestiza. I wasn't sure which attitude made me more uncomfortable—because I didn't know which way I felt, myself. Or which way I *wanted* to feel. I'm too much of an anthropologist to buy into the idea that blood wins out over culture, but at the same time, there was a part of me that wanted to belong, to lay claim to an identity as Macehualli, as one of them, by simple virtue of the fact that my abuela had been.

If Spanish was a pleasant surprise, English was an outright shock. I hadn't spoken the language in what felt like several lifetimes; hell, most of my notes were in Spanish or Nahuatl. When I met Dr. Westerfeld for lunch and she said, "Hi, Anita; how's your project going?," for a moment I could only gape at her as if she were speaking Klingon.

Her smile widened. "That good, huh? Have a seat."

Dr. Westerfeld wasn't my advisor; she was a UCLA archaeologist who happened to be working in the Huastecan region of Veracruz. Her dig was on the nearby Río Serpiente, so she'd offered to check in on me occasionally. I was pathetically grateful for the kindness. Even in these modern times, fieldwork was often a sink-or-swim experience, and my obsession with La Molejera and inability to learn anything about her had me afraid I was sinking. How many things had I failed to pay attention to, because I was thinking about her? How much damage might I do to my situation there, if they found out I had gone to see her? Doubt is an ever-present hobgoblin in the field, and I was tired of battling it. I wanted to pour all of my troubles out to Dr. Westerfeld, maybe cry a little in her lap. I wanted to call my advisor and beg *her* for help. I wanted to call mi mamá, and I would this afternoon, but she couldn't help me with this.

What I *really* wanted to do was talk to my abuela, but she was dead and gone.

As La Molejera, for some reason, was not.

I tried to put the old woman out of my mind. I made some noncommittal responses about my work in Chalchi, told a few stories about my language difficulties, got Dr. Westerfeld to laugh. I'd taken Classical Nahuatl in grad school, the only version of the language offered in a formal course; Dr. Westerfeld had been the one to teach me what she knew of the modern Hustequeño version of the language, so I wouldn't show up sounding like a refugee from the Aztec Empire.

"How's your dig going?" I asked her as the food finally arrived. "Any luck with Sister?"

Dr. Westerfeld nodded enthusiastically. "Tons. Bruce is still calling me every half hour, practically, checking in to make sure I haven't broken her or dropped her in the river, but we've been working her nonstop, and the results we're getting are fantastic."

The waiter must have understood English; I caught him giving her a startled look before he put his attention back on the dishes he was laying out. I swallowed a snicker. "Sister" was not a person; she was a machine, the Sub-Surface Imaging System, or SSIS. The brainchild of Dr. Westerfeld and Bruce Steinman, an engineer she was collaborating with at Caltech, SSIS was the latest innovation in remote sensing for archaeologists, making pictures of what was under the ground without digging it up first. She was also insanely expensive; from what I'd heard, Steinman had told Dr. Westerfeld she should let her whole crew die before she risked the slightest damage to Sister.

"Did some tests on structures, first," Dr. Westerfeld went on, oblivious to our waiter's reaction. He finished his work and left, casting one last glance back at her. "Now we've moved onto finer-grained testing—burials, in fact."

The way she said it clued me in that I was supposed to find this somehow important. I dragged my mind off its one-woman track and racked my memory. "Wait—I thought the practice back then was to cremate the dead, not bury them."

"It was," Dr. Westerfeld said, and the grin she'd been trying to suppress broke over her face. "Which makes this all the more incredible. For that alone, the Río Serpiente project has justified its existence. And then on top of that, there's something weird about the burials. Sister can't quite make out the details—we'd still have to dig them up to do pathological examinations or anything on that scale—but they show evidence of a practice I've never heard of *anywhere* before."

"What do you mean?"

"Removal of long bones, from every burial we've found."

I didn't know much about the time period Dr. Westerfeld was working with, although I needed to read up on it, as her research covered the time when the core ethnic group of the Aztec Empire, the ancestors of the Macehualli, migrated into lands originally held by the Huasteca. But I knew enough to find that odd. "*All* of the long bones?"

"No. A lot of the burials aren't well preserved, unfortunately— that's the tropics for you—but it looks like the femurs are gone. In juvenile burials as well as adult. There's traces of something where they should be; I want to excavate and see what they are. Looks like they might have had wooden posts put in place."

I had a sudden, bizarre image of Aztec pirates. "Peg legs?"

"In place of the *femurs?* With the lower leg still there? No, it has to have been done as some kind of funerary practice, after the person was already dead. Or at least that's my theory. I'd have to excavate to know more; could just be they decayed badly for some reason, and all that's left are bone stains Sister isn't going to pick up. Maybe there was something placed over the upper legs that dissolved the bone." Dr. Westerfeld shrugged and took a large bite out of a tamale, as if she talked about dead people over lunch every day. Which she probably did—archaeologists are like that. "It's been known to happen. Look at bog bodies."

I did not, in fact, want to look at bog bodies, whatever she meant by that. I was an anthropologist, not an archaeologist, because I preferred my research subjects to be *alive*. "Why would they take the femurs out?"

"No idea. Like I said, I've never heard of this before, not anywhere. It'll make a great research question for the future, though."

We continued to chat about our respective projects as we ate. Later, when I went back to Chalchi, I regretted that; while it had been nice to run some of my thoughts by someone else, maybe I should have used the time to think about something other than my project for once. But by the time I thought of that, I'd missed my chance.

After lunch I called my family, chatted with them for a short time—too short, but they were busy and I only had a limited time in Tuxpan. Then I went to the small room in the municipal building that had been loaned to me for the time being, and dug into my books.

I'd brought quite a few when I drove down from L.A., but most of them had stayed here in Tuxpan; it was just too difficult to haul them over the tortuous forest tracks that led to Chalchi. I'd written out a list of things I needed to look up in books I had foolishly decided to leave here, so I plugged in my little portable stereo that had also not made the trip and settled down to listen to music and do some reading.

I was right; Chicomexochitl *had* been an Aztec deity. I scribbled down a few notes on him, then paged idly through the book. No doubt when I went back over my field notes later I'd find more echoes lingering into modern times. For now, I just let my eyes glide over the pages. The previous "suns" or ages of the world. The creation of humans in this, the fifth sun, from the bones of the previous race. All the old gods, with their names full of snakes: Quetzalcoatl, Cihuacoatl, Coatlicue. Maybe Dr. Westerfeld had the right idea after all, studying dead people. At least they couldn't make you feel like you were an idiot but they were too polite to point it out, when you said something wrong or burned yet another tortilla. Seriously, I was beginning to wonder if I'd been born without the tortilla-making gene or something.

But that led me back to my questions about who I was, to these people or to myself, and I'd had enough of those.

So I did my reading, and went out drinking that night, and woke up hungover just in time to slog through the forests back to Chalchi.

Back to the questions I could not answer, and could not leave alone.

(excerpt from Chalchihuitlan field notes, 8/16)

Feather-boys in other villages, too. ??? Old widows supported

*by youngest sons, or other family. Usually. Why multiple
villages feeding one woman? Or do they have their own Las
Molejeras to feed?...*

*...All other villages with feather-boys are daughter villages of
Chalchi. Prob. carried tradition with when they split. But
why? Not necessary; why is it that important?*

In late August I was allowed to observe a funeral. Not everyone
wanted me there; the "Anita is not one of us" crowd argued
against it in the meeting of elders, I later heard. But the family of
the old man who had died were okay with me coming, and their
voices won out.

The Macehualli take funerals very seriously; if they don't treat
the dead properly, they leave themselves open to all kinds of
trouble from wind spirits and restless ghosts from *mictlan*, the
underworld. They allowed me to come, but not to bring a camera
or a tape recorder, so my experience of the event consisted of
long stretches of time where I struggled to stay awake against the
soporific effect produced by thick clouds of copal smoke and
slow, droning music, punctuated by spates of mad scribbling
when something finally happened and I had to try and write it all
down.

The deceased was an old man who had been very ill for a
long time; his relatives seemed torn between sadness and relief
that he was out of pain. It reminded me vividly of my own
abuela's funeral, even though the surroundings were wildly
different—the dark interior of the house, the copal incense, the
marigolds laid on the body and twisted into a garland leading up
to a roof-beam, forming a path for one piece of the multi-part
Macehualli soul to find its way free of the flesh. Abuela Rosa, too,
had been ill, and we'd been relieved for her sake, but I had cried
for weeks. And now, in the darkness of the house, that feeling
came back to me.

I tried to hold on to my tears, clinging to the myth of anthropological detachment, but as the hours wore on it grew harder and harder, and then another woman broke into high-pitched keening, and I lost it. There in the corner where I'd stuffed myself out of the way, I broke down and cried again for my abuela, with the scent of copal filling my head. And this isn't the kind of thing you can ever write in a dissertation, can't even admit professionally, but for a short while there, I was one of them. Not an outsider. I keened along with the women, for my abuela as much as for the poor old dead man lying on the floor with a white cloth over his face, and I felt like I belonged.

The moment passed. I dried my tears, picked up my pen, wrote down the chant the prayer-leader read. The last hours of the night passed, and when morning came, we took the body to be buried.

I almost lost it in a different way then. Light-headed with the incense and the lack of food, the disorientation of a night spent in ritual, I was a little unsteady on my feet. They brought in the cedar coffin, drew a cross in the bottom with white ashes, laid cloth over it, followed by a set of women's clothes for the wife they expected the old man to find in *mictlan*. But when they lifted the body into the coffin, something about the way it moved was just *wrong*. As they wrapped the marigold garland around the body, the legs flopped loosely in their white pants, undignified and grotesque, and I almost threw up in my corner. I'd been there when my abuela passed, asleep in her bed, and I'd seen her in her coffin, but not moving between the two. Shouldn't rigor mortis keep him stiff? Or had that passed already?

I regained my composure while they placed objects in the coffin with the body, then trailed along in their wake as they carried the coffin out of the house and to the graveyard. There was a hole already prepared, and the men made quick work of setting up a wooden platform over the coffin after they lowered it, so no dirt would fall directly on the box. They filled in the grave, we set up a cross and hung it with yet more marigolds, and the funeral was over.

As mourners began to disperse, I saw Pepe Rodríguez among

the assembled villagers. Not surprising; in the Macehualli way of things, it turned out that more than half of Chalchi was related to the old man in one way or another. Seeing Pepe, I had a sudden brainstorm, and contrived to drift over in his direction. I knew I should keep taking notes about the funeral, about what people did when the ceremony itself was over, but I didn't want to pass this chance up.

After all, nobody had more direct contact with La Molejera than the feather-boy. Who better to tell me about her than him? And children are easier to talk to, less close-mouthed than their parents.

All of them except this one, apparently.

Pepe shook his head when I came up, bypassing Macehualli indirection with all the straightforward, battering-ram charm of the young. "She told me not to talk to you."

I swallowed and revised my plan. "Doesn't your mother like me?"

"Not her," Pepe said, shifting to seven-year-old scorn at my blindness. "*Her.*"

The emphasis was unmistakable. "La Molejera spoke to you?"

For a moment, I thought I might be able to trick him into talking anyway. He caught himself at the last instant, though. "I'm not telling you anything. She'd be angry if I did." Quick as a snake, he ran away to join a small herd of other children.

I stared after him, feeling thwarted. It was such a good idea, too. Except that La Molejera apparently thought of it before I did.

Sighing, I gathered up the shreds of my anthropological discipline and went off to record the aftermath of the funeral.

(excerpt from Chalchihuitlan field notes, 9/1)

Tepecihuatl.

Didn't even hear it during the funeral; just scribbled it down.

Only noticed it now. Hill-woman. Thought it was just random spirit, but HAS to refer to La M. Fits context of chant.

Not even the only place she's mentioned! In half the chants! Checked old notes, seeing her everywhere now. Tepecihuatl, tepecoatl, tecimaitl, tlaquiz-tlalcihuatl, lots of names. Obsession is justified. Must have noticed it unconsciously. SHE'S at the CENTER of their religion, their rituals. Subtle, but there. (I'm NOT crazy. Not imagining it.)

Can't give up on figuring her out, then. Too important to understanding why Chalchi's held onto to old ways. Betting now they DO replace La M when she dies, so they always have one. But why?

I climb the hill a third time, since no one has told me not to, and in fact the indirect hints that I should stay away have begun to die off. I feel as if everyone knows I'm pursuing this, and is waiting to see what will happen.

I am, no doubt, imagining things, thanks to the stress and psychological weirdness of fieldwork. But that doesn't stop me from going.

At the top of the hill, I wait for the snakes to clear, trying to convince myself I'm less afraid of them than I used to be, and failing miserably. When they're gone, I wait a while longer, for politeness' sake, while La Molejera grinds her stone into powder, before going and seating myself in front of her, but a small distance away. I'm getting used to the skin-crawling feel.

"What does your heart say, grandmother?" I ask her, remembering this time to say hello in the proper way. She doesn't answer me, and I don't expect her to. I just sit and wait, with the sun pounding down on my head and the sound of her grinding vibrating in my bones.

I can't be sure, since I didn't look that closely on my previous visits, but it looks like she's got more unground stone in her metate than before. Bad timing on my part, then, as it means I've missed her refreshing her stock; I may have to wait a while until she does it again. How long does it take to grind a metate full of stone? Longer than corn, no doubt. I just hope it won't take her all day. She's ignoring me, but she hasn't given even the faintest hint that I should leave, so I plan to just sit and observe. I'm not even taking notes. I won't have trouble remembering what I see.

The time creeps by. Under the scrape of the mano, I hear slitherings that are probably snakes, but I stay where I am. The awful sound of the grinding doesn't get any less awful, but I get accustomed to it in a way, lulled almost into a trance, and so I don't jump out of my skin when she finally speaks.

"You have patience."

I don't jump, but it takes me a moment to sort through her words. Her Nahuatl is hard to understand, although my time in Chalchi has gotten me to the point where I can usually cope with it. The words of my response rise slowly to my tongue. "I am learning patience."

Scrape, scrape, scrape. I wonder if that's going to be the extent of our conversation. Just when I've given up on more, she speaks again. "Have you brought food for me?"

I haven't, and I kick myself for not thinking of it. "I'm sorry, grandmother, but no."

More grinding silence. Her hands are old and wrinkled, but they look strong, hardened by who knows how many years of this work. I open my mouth to ask, then shut it. I've made more progress this time than ever before, and it hasn't been by babbling at her. I'll wait.

I think another hour passes. I can't be sure. The sun moves overhead, but in the blazing light and heat I can't really track it. I brought a small bottle of water; it's already gone. Heat exhaustion, here I come.

"For what do you wait?" she asks, and a small piece of stone cracks under her mano with the snap of a broken bone.

Information. Answers. Understanding.

"I don't know."

"Why wait without purpose?"

I have a purpose, yet I told the truth when I said I didn't know what it was. I risk asking her a question myself. "For what do *you* wait?"

"For the next one."

Next anthropologist? Next La Molejera? Next visit from the feather-boy? But we've lapsed back into silence again, and then the back of my neck prickles, and I look up to see doña Magdalena at the head of the path, her hands resting on the shoulders of little Pepe. He has no food with him, either; I notice this, irrationally, because I'm afraid doña Magdalena is going to be angry.

I murmur a farewell to La Molejera, who takes no notice, and go with doña Magdalena.

Pepe scoots off down the path ahead of us, mission apparently accomplished. I walk with the other woman in silence for a while. Compared to the silence of La Molejera's hilltop, this one is lightweight, breathable, *human*. In the shade of the trees, I blink and try to get my vision back.

"Now you understand," doña Magdalena says at last.

I don't understand a damn thing. I open my mouth to say so, look sideways at her, and swallow it. She's not angry, because she thinks I've learned whatever I was supposed to. Telling her I haven't may put us where I feared we would be.

"Yes," I tell her, and flinch at the lie.

She nods. "Good." And we walk the rest of the way in silence.

(excerpt from Chalchihuitlan field notes, 9/10)

I know why I had a hard time understanding her.

She wasn't speaking Huastecan Nahuatl.

She was speaking Classical.

The days after that drifted by in an ordinary routine of fieldwork. The various debates about me seemed to have faded out entirely; I was Macehualli now. Because I understood La Molejera.

Or so they thought.

I hoped for a while that I might be able to figure out what I had missed through conversation; now that they thought I understood, maybe they would talk about it in front of me. No such luck. La Molejera, apparently, was one of those things so fundamental to the culture that nobody *needed* to talk about her. Which made it all the more crucial that I understand what she meant to them, why she was there. And now I might have shot my only chance of doing so.

I turned to my data in the hope of finding a key there. I had reams of notes on rituals, and was gathering reams more. I remembered the days when I first came to Chalchi, how long I'd had to wait before María Francisca let me come to that first curing ritual, and almost missed the free time; now, if I didn't show up for a ritual, more often than not they'd send a kid to fetch me.

It wasn't hard to spot the references to La Molejera in the chants for the rituals, now that I knew what to look for. But, in the usual way of ritual language, the chants didn't come out and say anything directly. She was the woman on the hill, the patient one, the one who worked. She waited. For what? Her hill was sacred—big surprise; half the landscape was sacred in one way or another. She didn't seem to be a shaman; the way the chants referred to her was the way they referred to spirits. But the definition of "spirit" was flexible.

Now I was more afraid than ever of doing something wrong. When I'd arrived in the village I'd made all kinds of mistakes, but they'd been excused on the grounds that I was ignorant and an outsider. Now I was assumed to be neither, and that meant I had less leeway for screwing up.

I took notes, and observed, and lay awake long into the night, unable to sleep for the questions rattling endlessly through my mind.

Bad news came to the village one day. A young man named Luis had turned up dead—murdered. Rumor said he'd been killed by workers on a ranch that bordered Chalchi's territory; conflicts with ranchers were far from uncommon, as Macehualli and mexicanos competed for scarce land. The death of the old man in August had been expected, and in its way a mercy. This was something different, and people feared it might lead to trouble.

Before anything could happen, though, Luis had to be buried, lest his spirit cause its own kind of trouble for the village.

I'd been at the old man's funeral, but only after the body was prepared and laid out in the house of his family. This time, Luis's little sister came around to ask me if I'd like to come see them prepare the body. My knee-jerk reaction was a visceral "hell, no"—funerals were bad enough—but I looked at her solemn face, its usual smile gone, and I said yes. It was a generous gesture, and I didn't want to offend.

"Can you find your way?" she asked as we left the small house that had been given over to me. "I need to fetch Pepe, too."

"Yes," I said. The irregular geography of Chalchi had confused me when I first came, with houses tucked away in odd pockets of the forest, but I'd learned my way around by now.

She thanked me and trotted off, leaving me to go to her family's house alone. And only then did I notice what else she had said: that she needed to find Pepe.

I chewed on possible meanings for that as I automatically took the correct paths through the trees. Why Pepe? Children helped out on all kinds of things, yes, and not everything he did had to do with La Molejera—but was this really random chance?

A flash of light caught my eyes through the last screen of vegetation separating me from the house compound.

I stopped where I was on the path, looking at it, and had just enough time to identify it as sun glinting off the blade of the machete all adult men in Chalchi carried, before it sliced downward with a sound I'd heard before, on those rare occasions when villagers butchered animals for meat.

My feet carried me forward, one resisting step at a time, to the very edge of the trees.

Luis's body was stretched out on the ground, naked and bloody, and his elder brother had just finished cutting out his right thigh. As I watched, hands pressed to my mouth as if that would stop me being sick, the machete flashed again and cut off his left leg. A moment later, the left thigh was severed as well. The brother handed the pieces of meat to another man, a cousin one corner of my mind identified reflexively, who wrapped them in a thick piece of cloth and set them aside.

I sank to my knees on the path, just shy of the edge of the house compound, and watched through the curtain of leaves as they washed the blood from Luis's mutilated body and bandaged the remaining pieces of his legs. Then they dressed the body, pulling a shirt on against the resistance of the stiffening arms, buttoning it up, all with solemn, grieving faces, totally at odds with the violence they had committed against their kinsman's corpse.

Before they put trousers on what remained of his lower body, though, they brought out two pieces of wood, and put them in place of the missing femurs.

Just like Dr. Westerfeld had described.

My sudden wild speculations on continuity of funerary practices from ancient times to the present didn't have time to filter upward through my barely-suppressed urge to vomit. There was new movement up ahead; from another path to the compound, little Pepe Rodríguez, the feather-boy, darted into view.

The cousin put the bundle of butchered human flesh into his arms, and murmured something I could not hear.

I was moving before I knew it. Months in Chalchi had taught me all the paths, and the places that weren't quite paths but you could get through them if you really needed to; I knew how to move quickly.

And I knew where Pepe was going.

(excerpt from Chalchihuitlan field notes, 8/11)

Spanish term: chico de plumas, feather-boy. Nahuatl term: quetzalconej.

Quetzalcoatl = *Feathered Snake*

I slow when I see him on the path ahead of me, duck behind a tree in case he looks back. He doesn't. He's trotting up the hill with the heavy bundle in his arms, little face bright as he carries out his sacred duty.

I follow, at a distance, because I must see.

The snakes do not leave when Pepe arrives, nor when I conceal myself at the end of the path, but I have no eyes for them. All my attention is on the old woman, La Molejera, grinding away in her metate.

As Pepe approaches, she lays down her mano, and the sound stops.

He sets the bundle on the ground in front of her and unwraps it. The smell of bloody meat fills the air.

La Molejera reaches out with her strong, wrinkled hands, and lifts the thigh of poor murdered Luis. As she opens her mouth, I see that her teeth are not an old woman's teeth. They are strong and white and sharp.

Nor is her eating is a human eating. The meat vanishes too rapidly, gulped down in quick, tearing bites. She strips the bone clean, then starts on the other, and when she is done the bones are white and dry.

And I see her for what she is.

She is taller, younger, fiercer. Her face is painted half red, half black, skull-like and staring beneath the pigment. On her arm is a shield decorated with eagle feathers. Serpents twine to form her skirt.

She takes the long bones and turns back to her metate. She places them in among the fragments and powder there, strikes them with her mano. They crack with a dull sound. As she grips the mano and begins her work once more, my vision of her true face fades, and all I see is the old woman, La Molejera, grinding not stone, but bone.

(excerpt from the Leyenda de los Soles [The Legend of the Suns], trans. John Bierhorst)

[At the beginning of the fifth sun]

And then the gods talked to each other and said, "Who will there be?"...

...Then Quetzalcoatl went to the dead land, and when he came to the dead land lord, the dead land lady, he said to him, "I've come for the precious bones that you are keeping. I've come to get them."

Then he said, "To do what, Quetzalcoatl?"

And he answered him, "It's because the gods are sad. Who will there be on earth?"...

...Then he takes the precious bones. The male bones are in one pile, the female bones are in another pile. Then Quetzalcoatl takes them, wraps them up, and comes carrying them off....

...Then he carried them to Tamoanchan. And when he had brought them, the one named Quilaztli, Cihuacoatl, ground them up. Then she put them into a jade bowl...

...Then they said, "Holy ones, humans, have been born."

What do I say now? Or do I say anything at all? I know who and what La Molejera is. I know what she waits for. I've read the myth over and over again, going back to my office in Tuxpan, pleading illness as my reason for leaving Chalchi so abruptly. I said it was temporary, but I don't know if I can go back.

Do I react as an anthropologist would, and document this fascinating practice for all the world to gape over? Do I react as a mestiza would, and denounce the barbaric habits of the Indian peasants? Do I react as most Americans would, and refuse to believe that what I have seen is real?

Or do I react as the Macehualli would, as the people of Chalchi do?

I am not one of them. I will not live out my life in Chalchi, die there, and have my long bones cut from my body to feed La Molejera and provide material for her grinding. I will not be the dust from which the next race of people is made. But I have spent too long among the people of Chalchi to divide myself from them, either.

How do I write about what I have seen? Or do I write at all?

'The Place of Jade':
Echoes of the Aztec Past in the Religion of Chalchihuitlan

by Anita Muñoz

Submitted to the faculty
of the University of California at Los Angeles
in partial fulfillment of the requirements for the degree of
Doctor of Philosophy
in the Department of Anthropology

I sit at my desk, day after day, staring at a picture of a statue of Cihuacoatl, and I can still hear her. Across two thousand intervening miles I hear her, sitting on her hill in the forests of Veracruz, grinding the bones of the human race, waiting for the end of this sun and the beginning of the next.

And I wonder how soon it will come.

Comparison of Efficacy Rates for Seven Antipathetics as Employed Against Lycanthropes

Abstract

This study seeks to establish a hierarchy of efficacy for various antipathetic materials and delivery mechanisms thereof as used in the extermination of lycanthropes. Pre-existing data on this issue consists solely of folkloric narratives and unsubstantiated anecdotes on Internet communities, neither of which are based upon suitable experimental trials. It is hoped that this study will be only the beginning of a proper body of scientific literature, which might be expanded to include hyena men, were-jaguars, and other therianthropes.

Definition

For the purpose of this study, a lycanthrope is a human being who physically transforms into a lupine or hybrid lupine-hominid shape, acquiring greater strength, speed, and reduced vulnerability to ordinary weapons. Available evidence indicates that this alteration is linked to the lunar cycle, though a full explication of the mechanism of transformation and its contagious nature awaits further study.

Violent aggression is not a necessary part of the definition, but seems to be either an ancillary effect of lycanthropy, or a co-morbid condition with it. Anecdotal reports of friendly lycanthropes are at present unsubstantiated.

METHODOLOGY

Numerous difficulties present themselves in any attempt to scientifically test the folklore regarding materials antipathetic to lycanthropes. Foremost among these is the lack of acceptance within the scientific community as to the existence of lycanthropy, beyond the psychiatric condition; this severely limits funding, peer review, and institutional support.

Because of this lack, it proved impossible to test antipathetics under laboratory conditions. The capture and maintenance of one caged specimen, much less several, was judged to be both dangerous and prohibitively expensive. The study therefore proceeded instead via field trials. Through the online community[1], the investigator contacted individuals who had expressed the intention of hunting lycanthropes in the immediate future. These subjects were each provided with a different antipathetic or delivery mechanism thereof, and each expressed his or her willingness to allow the investigator to document the hunt.

In most cases, the field trials were recorded by means of head-mounted night-vision cameras, worn by the experimental subject, which streamed video wirelessly to the investigator's computer. On occasion it proved feasible to set up a stationary camera. These recordings were supplemented by the investigator's own notes, and (where possible) exit interviews with the hunters.

This research was not authorized by a Human Subjects Committee or other ethics review board.

1

Including the websites Wolfpelt, Lunar Eclipse, and Sisterhood of the Silver Bullets.

TRIAL 1: ARGENT PROJECTILE (MODERN)

The metallurgy of silver makes it difficult to manufacture silver bullets suitable for use in a modern firearm[2]. The investigator secured the use of a university metallurgy lab and the assistance of a professional firearms manufacturer to produce eighteen .357 caliber rounds[3], or two clips for a Desert Eagle pistol. The first subject, Hunter A, was a thirty-six-year-old male with a career in law enforcement, whose wife had recently been disemboweled by a lycanthrope. After demonstrating his firearms accuracy so as to establish a baseline for comparison, he commenced the search for his target[4].

Lycanthrope A was discovered consuming the corpse of a small child in a dead-end urban alley. Hunter A positioned himself at the mouth of the alley, approximately thirty meters from the target, while the investigator observed from the other side of the cross-street, concealed behind a newspaper dispenser. Video data shows that Hunter A's shots exhibited 64% less accuracy than in the baseline demonstration: he had previously declared his

---

[2]Briggs 2005: http://www.patriciabriggs.com/books/silver/silverbullets.shtml.

[3]

Thirty rounds were produced in total; twelve were eliminated due to poor quality, which would have increased the risk of gun malfunction in the field and therefore biased the data. This production issue, however, must be considered relevant to the larger question of efficacy. (For ballistics information on this ammunition, see the appendix.)

[4]

For a full account of each subject's background, involvement in the anti-lycanthrope community, and predatory efforts, see the author's monograph *Under the Full Moon: An Urban Safari Into the Biology of Lycanthropes*, in preparation.

intention to aim for the head[5], but of the six shots he fired, two
flew wide to the left, three flew wide to the right, and one struck
Lycanthrope A in the shoulder. Hunter A attempted to fire a
seventh shot, but suffered a gun malfunction, and then was struck
to the ground by the charging lycanthrope. It is notable, however,
that the lycanthrope fled rather than engage in further confrontation.

Retrieval and examination of the pistol shows that the seventh
round did not chamber correctly, owing to the separation of the
silver point from its copper case. The decrease in accuracy may
arise from multiple causes, including fear-induced operator error.
It may be presumed, however, that the difficulty of casting high-
quality silver bullets introduces a degree of variability which will
decrease performance under field conditions, even where malfunction does not occur.

The escape of Lycanthrope A unfortunately precluded the
possibility of forensic examination. Six spent bullets, however—
one bloodstained—were recovered from the test location; this
indicates that the shot which struck the target's shoulder passed
through the tissue and out the other side. The investigator observed
a distinct limp and other indications of pain as the lycanthrope
fled (the video camera by this time was recording the pavement),
which suggests a genuine injury to the target.

TRIAL 2: ARGENT PROJECTILE (ARCHAIC)

The difficulty of casting silver bullets to the exacting specifications
of modern firearms suggests that archaic weapons might prove
more efficacious, when the variables of performance are weighed
against those of manufacture. The investigator therefore secured
the assistance of a professional silversmith, who produced twelve
balls suitable for use in an eighteenth-century musket.

---

[5]While it may lie beyond the scope of this study to make
tactical evaluations of lycanthrope-hunting techniques, the
investigator believes it is generally more advisable to aim for
the center mass, for reasons illustrated by Hunter A's results.

Hunter B was a twenty-two-year-old female with experience in American Revolutionary War re-enactment, whose boyfriend vanished during a camping trip in the mountains. As with Hunter A, she demonstrated her skill with a replica period weapon before beginning her search. In this instance, the investigator remained at camp, inside an SUV with the engine running and pointed toward the road.

Video data for this trial is non-continuous, due to the problems of wireless transmission in mountainous terrain. On the third night Hunter B observed her target, Lycanthrope B, drinking water from a stream. Unfortunately, she made her observation from a hillside well beyond the range of a musket, and by the time she moved closer, Lycanthrope B had vanished. Subject and investigator therefore returned to that area the following month, and this time Hunter B met with success on the first night. She found her target howling at the moon on a bare hilltop, and the yelping end of the howl indicates that her first shot struck home, though it is not possible from the recording to determine where Lycanthrope B was wounded. The target fled, however, before Hunter B could reload her musket. No limp was discernible on this occasion, which may indicate that the lesser muzzle velocity of an archaic firearm caused the projectile to penetrate less deeply than in Trial 1. Upon returning to the hilltop in daylight, Hunter B found little sign of blood, which corroborates this speculation.

The trial could not be continued on the following night due to the disappearance of Hunter B.

TRIAL 3: ARGENT SHOT

The investigator pursued one further solution to the difficulty of silver bullets, in the form of shot. Silver beads were obtained from a craft store, and placed in a shotgun cartridge in lieu of the customary lead shot. The firearm in this instance was a Remington 870 pump-action shotgun.

Hunter C was a fifty-seven-year-old male with over forty years of hunting experience. His six-year-old son had been fatally mauled the previous summer on Hunter C's ranch. The subject

declined to undergo a formal demonstration of his marksman-
ship, despite explanations of its value for research, but did feed
the investigator a dinner cooked from a pheasant he brought
down with his shotgun.

Data from this trial consists solely of the investigator's notes,
as Hunter C likewise declined use of the head-mounted camera or
other video-recording equipment. On the first night of the full
moon he staked a female sheep in the open ground twenty meters
beyond his barn, having first cut the animal with a knife, so the
scent of its blood would draw the predator. He then waited inside
the open barn door, with the investigator behind a hay bale. This
having produced no results, on the second night he cut the ewe's
throat and staked a lamb next to her, declaring that the greater
quantity and the cries of the lamb would be more effective.

Methods of luring lycanthropes are outside the scope of this
study, but on that night Lycanthrope C appeared. Hunter C
immediately left the concealment of the barn and began walking
toward his target, firing as he went. Lycanthrope C was observed
to flinch slightly at each shot, and the investigator believes the
subject's aim was good, but the small quantities of silver seemed
to do little more than irritate the target. Hunter C continued
approaching even after running out of ammunition, dry-firing and
shouting with incoherent grief, and subsequently fell victim to
the lycanthrope.

The lamb was unharmed.

TRIAL 4: ARGENT BLADE

The investigator next obtained a silver-plated bowie knife. While
the lesser hardness of pure silver (as compared to carbon steel or
stainless steel) would ordinarily render it unsuitable for use in a
bladed weapon, the antipathetic nature of silver is hypothesized
to counterbalance this deficiency.

Hunter D was a twenty-two-year-old male gang member who

had lost his younger brother to a lycanthrope[6]. Although it was not possible to obtain quantitative data regarding his proficiency with the weapon, as with Hunters A and B, other informants corroborated his statement that he was the victor in four previous knife fights.

In this instance the hunt was organized as a planned encounter between Hunter D and Lycanthrope D. The investigator was therefore able to position a stationary camera on a fire escape above the agreed-upon location, in lieu of the head-mounted camera Hunter D could not wear. The ideal nature of this setup, unfortunately, was compromised when friends of Hunter D refused to allow the investigator to monitor events from a safe distance via the computer. This field trial was therefore observed at close range, with notes recorded afterward.

This ultimately proved to be only a minor limitation. Measured from the moment the combatants approached each other to the moment when Hunter D's body struck the ground, the confrontation lasted for 3.6 seconds. Hunter D thrust the knife into Lycanthrope D's side, approximately in the location where the spleen would be located in a fully human body, whereupon Lycanthrope D tore Hunter D's head from his body[7]. While the silver does appear to have wounded the target satisfactorily—

---

[6]

Initially this subject was disqualified from the trial on the basis of evidence that he was merely seeking revenge against the non-lycanthropic leader of a rival gang. The alternative candidate for the fourth trial, however, revoked her permission and abandoned her hunt at the same time that new evidence came to light, supporting Hunter D's claim regarding his target. (It is regrettable that this new evidence took the form of an entire gang of lycanthropes.)

[7]

This analysis is based on slow-motion playback of the video recording. The investigator failed to directly observe anything of value either during the confrontation or after, as safety considerations required immediate departure from the trial location.

Lycanthrope D was heard to howl in pain when it removed the blade—the necessity of close approach renders this method inadvisable.

TRIAL 5: $AGNO_3$

This particular trial was suggested by Hunter E, a forty-one-year-old female with over a decade's experience as a zookeeper. The investigator observed her on a message board suggesting that lycanthropes might be hunted with tranquilizer guns. Although the efficacy of sedatives and paralytics in this context is highly dubious, the darts could be adapted to deliver other compounds.

Together with Hunter E, the investigator conducted a preliminary series of experiments with modified darts. Colloidal silver, unfortunately, showed a tendency to clog the bore of the needle. Instead two syringes of silver nitrate were prepared: one with a standard steel needle, and one with a specially-crafted silver needle.

Hunter E had suffered no personal encounter with lycanthropes, and so had no immediate target. The investigator therefore introduced her to the city district occupied by the lycanthrope gang. Together they chose a suitable target, one who appeared to be an outcast member of the pack. This target was lured to an alley by means of fresh lamb chops, obtained from a nearby butcher. A stationary camera was again positioned on a fire escape, in addition to the head-mounted camera worn by the subject. The investigator observed from a parked car nearby.

Equipped with a night scope, Hunter E sighted on the target from a distance of twenty-seven meters and fired the steel-needle syringe. This produced a confused and wary reaction from the target, but no sign of incapacity or pain. Hunter E loaded the silver-needle syringe and fired a second time, whereupon Lycanthrope E fled the scene.

Examination afterward revealed that the silver needle bent slightly on impact, closing off the bore and preventing the silver nitrate from being expelled. Traces of blood on the tip show that it did penetrate the flesh, to a depth of approximately half a centimeter; video analysis suggests the dart fell out of Lycanthrope E's shoulder soon after contact. The steel-needle syringe appears to have bounced off the target without penetration. The efficacy of silver nitrate therefore remains unknown.

Trial 6: Sorbus Aucuparia

The wood of this tree, commonly known as rowan or mountain ash, is well-documented in folklore as an antipathetic for witches, fairies, and werewolves. It is unsuitable for bullets of any sort, and the preceding trials suggested that both shot and melee weapons would be inadvisable. A trap was deemed the most appropriate delivery mechanism for the antipathetic.

By the time an appropriate quantity of material had been shipped to the investigator, a number of possible subjects had suggested themselves, all in the vicinity of Trials 4 and 5. Hunter F was a nineteen-year-old male, and the leader of one half of the surviving gang of which Hunter D had been a member. When provided with a book on survival techniques, including the crafting of pit traps, he and his companions[8] arranged twelve fire-hardened spikes of *S. aucuparia* inside a street-level delivery hatch to the basement of a nearby building. They then covered the opening with a tarp and sent their fastest runner, a fourteen-year-old male (henceforth called Assistant F), to lure a target toward the field site.

Hunter F declined to allow the investigator to place a stationary camera, or to equip any of the participants with head-mounted devices. It proved possible, however, for the investigator to slip one on in the moments preceding the commencement of the trial. The following data is based upon that recording.

The lure returned mixed results. Sounds issuing from outside the camera's field of view indicated that Assistant F was caught

---

[8] The investigator indicated to Hunter F that the trial would be biased if multiple subjects were directly involved. He responded in language unsuited to an academic journal.

and dispatched just beyond the mouth of the alley. Another individual (Assistant F2, male, age unknown) ran to his aid, but reversed course almost immediately, pursued by Lycanthrope F at a range of approximately two meters. Assistant F2, a heavily-built young man, appears to have lacked the dexterity of the late Assistant F; he missed his footing on the plank bridging the pit trap and fell in. Lycanthrope F immediately attempted to change course, but skidded on wet pavement and slid over the edge. Hunter F, along with Assistants F3-F7 (all male, ages unknown) ran to the pit trap, where they began throwing objects at Lycanthrope F and stamping on its hands[9] in an attempt to make it fall. This succeeded after approximately seven seconds, but the target missed the spikes; it only cracked one, and subsequently[10] ran off into the basement.

The efficacy of *S. aucuparia* against lycanthropes therefore remains dubious. Against human beings, however, the spikes proved quite fatal.

TRIAL 7: ACONITUM NAPELLUS

The role of the final antipathetic is suggested by its common name[11], wolfsbane. The most suitable delivery mechanism would seem to be a tranquilizer dart, but the unsatisfactory results of

---

[9]

Some lycanthropes observed in this study appear to have possessed opposable thumbs, but in other cases this trait is uncertain at best. There may be variation in the wild.

[10]

According to a report from Assistant F6; unverified by the investigator

[11]

One of many common names for the genus. Others include monkshood, aconite, blue rocket, and women's bane. No antipathetic qualities have been observed in human females—beyond the naturally-occurring cardiac poison, which is equally effective against human males.

Trial 5 ruled out this approach. The investigator considered stuffing lumps of meat with leaves of *A. napellus*, before concluding that the likelihood of persuading a lycanthrope to consume the meat was low. An infusion of the whole plant therefore seemed the most reliable means.

Hunter G is a twenty-four-year-old female graduate student in biology. No recording was made of the seventh trial, except for notes transcribed by the subject after the event. An infusion of *A. napellus* was prepared by the subject upon the arrival of Lycanthrope G[12] during daylight hours, in the period of the waning moon. When served to Lycanthrope G in a teacup and consumed by the target, it proved fatal within nine minutes. The efficacy of *A. napellus* against lycanthropes in their lupine or hybrid forms is still undocumented, but the howls and snarls of Lycanthrope G suggest that it operated upon more than simply the normal human cardiac function of the target.

CONCLUSION AND FURTHER STUDY

All the tested antipathetics and delivery mechanisms showed flaws that mar their efficacy. (Those which failed to produce any result may be deemed inefficacious by their general unreliability.) The most harm was inflicted by the modern argent projectile, the argent blade, and *A. napellus*, but the former suffers from difficulty of manufacture and unreliable performance, the second requires hazardous proximity to a lycanthrope, and the latter, thus far, has only proved its use against lycanthropes in human form.

Nevertheless, it is the opinion of Hunter G, in her role as investigator, that *A. napellus* offers the most promising avenue for further inquiry. Another course of field trials is intended, these testing the efficacy of an infusion of *A. napellus* applied externally, as delivered by a high-powered water gun. Trials 4, 5, and 6 have produced an abundance of suitable research targets, many of

---

12

Formerly known as Hunter B.

whom have demonstrated a tendency to approach the investigator of their own accord.

It is hoped that the documentation provided by this study will encourage others to pursue the topic of lycanthropic biology. There is an urgent need for a greater understanding of the subject, particularly in the vicinity of Philadelphia.

THE LAST WENDY

THE STARS WINKED in conspiratorial excitement as the two travelers flew by, borne on nighttime winds. Far below, the lights of London blazed with the unrelenting life of the city, broken only by the dark ribbon of the Thames. Every year London grew larger, stretching arms of concrete and wire into the green fields that encircled it, but the central areas stayed much the same, held in place by the weight of the past. And the travelers had eyes only for the familiar, disregarding with casual indifference the changes wrought by time.

The streets slipped by, shadowed and quiet, until a well-known roof came into view. The bay window on the top floor jittered and then swung open, hinges protesting quietly. In blew the evening breeze, carrying a dancing litter of leaves, and with it came two figures.

One flitted about, casting an unpredictable light over the room, expressing through movement her irritation with this journey. The other alit on the floor with the fleet and careless grace of the young. Ignoring his companion's vexation, he planted his hands on his hips and looked around.

The high, vaulted ceiling with its chipped and peeling frieze of vines, the lined expanse of the old wooden floor, the bay window he had come through so many times before—these were sights he took for granted, not so much trusting they would be there as assuming it, never giving the matter any thought at all, for in his mind, everything waited on him and did not change when he went away. Of course things *had* changed, more than once, but he forgot those times more swiftly than dawn forgot the night.

So he told himself, as he looked about, that there had only ever been the one bed, against the left-hand wall, and that the echoing space of the remaining area was quite as it should be. No embers glowed in the dusty fireplace (but after all, the spring air was warm) and no nightlight broke the darkness (but they always yawned themselves to sleep when he came).

On bare and sun-browned feet, he crept over to the bed, a kiss tucked into one hand.

He was an imaginative boy, capable of creating feasts upon which he would glut himself, feasts composed of airy nothings finer than any cook's delicacies. By the power of his imagination, he shaped the world around him, and so he came to this room entirely confident of finding what he expected.

With a chill quite unlike any he had forgotten, he found the bed empty.

His companion was still darting around, investigating the half-open drawers of the dresser and the clothes spilling from them, the clutter strewn across the dresser-top, the pictures pinned to the walls.

"Tink," said the boy, confused, "there's no one here."

Her twinkling response was equal parts satisfaction and resentment, for however pleased she was to find their target missing, she did not like coming all this way to find it.

He went to the window, questioning, for the first time, whether he had come to the wrong place. But the window was familiar, and the fireplace behind him, and outside was the street; this house was number fourteen, and this room its nursery.

He turned back, but the bed was still empty.

In the light spilling in from the street, he could just make out some things in the room. The covers on the bed were rumpled, as if the occupant had left them for a moment, or as if no one had bothered to make them in the morning. The pictures on the walls were not painted and framed, but rather simple sheets of paper stuck up with tape and small pins, and they showed dark, angry people in dark, angry scenes. The clothes held little color, lit by the hovering, flittering light of Tink above, but they gleamed with many bits of metal. Nowhere did he see a nightlight, or toys, or any of the things he associated with this place.

"Tink," the boy said again, "I don't understand."

The fairy might have responded, but they both jerked into wary postures at the sound of a footstep on the stair. No doubt the walker was doing his best to be quiet, but the staircase was very old indeed, and besides, the boy and the fairy spent their days evading Indians and pirates. Tink dove into the dark fabrics of the dresser, and the boy hid behind a stack of boxes in the corner.

The nursery door swung open to admit a small, shadowy figure who slipped through and shut it with stealth and care. At first the only visible detail of the figure was short hair, standing up in stiff little spikes, but as he noticed the window was open and went to shut it, the light from the streets illuminated his face and showed him to be not a boy at all, but a girl.

Perhaps this sight caused the boy to twitch behind the boxes, or perhaps the topmost box decided to help matters along on its own, for it toppled to the floor with an astonishing crash.

Boy and girl alike jumped in surprise, but it was the girl who spoke first, staring at the intruder thus revealed.

"Who the hell are *you?*" she demanded.

These were not the words he had expected of her, though of course he was not crying, and so it would have been odd of her to ask why he was doing so. But he felt a dislocation at her harsh question, crystallizing his heretofore vague sensation that something was badly out of joint.

"Hullo, Wendy," he said tentatively, trying to put matters back as they should be.

"Look, fucker—did you climb in through the window? Because I'm gonna call the police. They'll throw you in jail. I'll tell them you came up here to molest me—" And then her words cut off, for the boy came forward, into the moonlight, and she saw how young he was.

"My name is Peter Pan," he said.

She stared at him for a long, uncomfortable moment, not saying anything. Then she gave a bark of laughter that didn't sound amused at all. "Pull the other one."

He wasn't sure what she meant by that, but took refuge in the manners he had learned from fairy ceremonies. Offering her a grand and courteous bow, he said, "What is your name?"

"It sure as hell isn't Wendy," the girl said. "Whoever you're looking for, shithead, she isn't here. Why don't you jump out the window and go find her?" The girl's hand was stuffed into one pocket of her dark, metal-studded clothes, as if she held something tightly in one fist. Peter doubted it was a kiss.

She certainly was not Wendy. A part of his mind remembered, in a swift passage that would not allow him to dwell on it, that Wendy had grown up and gotten married and then...gone away. But there had been another Wendy, or rather Jane, the daughter of the first Wendy. And then Margaret, who was Jane's daughter, for the girls did not stay in the Neverland, where they would be safe from ever growing up. But they came to the Neverland for spring-cleaning every year.

Every year that Peter remembered to come for them.

"Are you Margaret?" he asked. She did not look much like Margaret, but changes happened—though never to him.

"Like I'm going to give you my name! You've got about five seconds to leave before I start screaming."

Peter came forward a few steps more. "Don't you know me?" he asked, and a plaintive note entered his voice—an injured note. He could imagine many things, but not insignificance. Not for himself. "I've come to take you to the Nev—"

His words dissolved into an outraged howl as the girl brought her hand out of her pocket and sprayed something in his face. The sensation was like nothing Peter had ever felt, not even when a skunk drenched him one time. His eyes watered and burned. This boy, who had fought pirates and Indians and crocodiles without showing a trace of fear, stumbled blind and crying about the room, until the glittering light of Tinker Bell flew to the window and called for him there. Away they flashed, through the air and up into the nighttime sky, leaving the nursery and its occupant behind.

Angie threw off her clothes as quick as she could and dove into bed. Not a moment too soon; she heard footsteps on the stairs, and then her father burst in, turning on the light and flooding the room with brightness.

"What's going on?" he cried, looking about. "Angie, what on earth—"

"There was someone at the window," she said, and pointed where it still hung open. "I saw someone, I swear, climbing in. But I yelled and he went away."

Her father rushed to the window and looked out, but by then there was nothing to see: just a light weaving erratically through the sky, to which he paid no attention.

"Are you sure?" he asked, turning back to his daughter. "It didn't sound like your voice. Was this one of your friends? Were you out again tonight?"

"No, I swear! I don't know who he was. Some kind of burglar, probably. He woke me up."

Angie's father searched the entire house, making sure nothing was missing, and scoured the tiny grounds as well. But he found no sign of the intruder, and when the window was securely latched again—this time with a box wedged against it—he left his daughter alone.

She tried to go to sleep, but dawn came tapping on her window before slumber did.

The alley behind the Indian take-away stank of curry, but it was out of sight of the street, where a passing copper might notice a clutch of kids not in school. The owner knew they were back there, but he wouldn't report them; he knew Angie could always tell the police about the business he conducted out his back door.

Angie's mate Josh took a deep drag out of the joint they were passing around and said, "Angie, chill out, would you? Singh ain't gonna report us."

She jerked her gaze away from the sky, and they all stared at her. She hadn't told them about the intruder; the truth was too weird, and too unnerving to lie around convincingly. The impossibility of it hovered in her mind, getting in the way of her thoughts.

"What if—" she began, voicing by accident the things she didn't want to say. Angie checked herself sharply, looking from Josh to Ollie to Dan. They'd think she was mad, or making shit up.

But she had started; she had to say *something*. "What if you could go anywhere?" she asked. "Blow off this shit, and just run away, or fly—" Hell. "Anywhere. Where would you go?"

"Glasgow," Ollie said instantly, nodding his pierced head decisively. "My brother's got a job there, fixing cars, souping them up for street racing. I'd go do that, too."

Dan, leaning back against the concrete wall, snorted in derision. "Why *work*, man? I'd go to Amsterdam, get high, never come down."

They promptly started an argument about the relative merits of Glasgow and Amsterdam, until Angie hissed at them to keep their voices down. She wished she had never asked. It was a dumb question, born of uncertainty and midnight confusion. But as the argument petered out, she realized Josh had never answered, and despite herself she looked at him.

He was sitting quietly, fiddling with the joint. Feeling their eyes on him, he shrugged. "I dunno," he said, and passed the joint to Dan. "Nowhere, I suppose. What would I go somewhere else for? I've got what I want, right here."

He set the other boys to arguing again, but not Angie. Her gaze crept, against her will, back to the sky.

But there was no one there.

Angie's father was at the kitchen table when she came home, hunched over the books that tallied their accounts. Columns and rows of tiny numbers in a tidy hand, with never a hint of the desperation behind them, the ever-present need to squeeze out just a little more: pay one more bill, hold off the creditors one more day. Angie hated the sight of him at the table, but she'd been hoping for it; Dad never had any attention to spare when he was doing the books.

"Hey Dad?" she called from the front hall.

She hesitated too long; if she'd asked her question quickly, like it was nothing important, her father would have answered without thinking. But she paused for a moment, long enough for him to surface from his dreary work and say, "Yes, Angie?"

If she said "nothing," it would just make him suspicious, and probably spark the questions she didn't want him asking, about why she hadn't been in school yet again. Where she'd been. What she'd been doing. Better to just say it now, before he got a chance.

"Where's Mum's old stuff?"

"Um. I don't know," he said vaguely; from his tone, he'd gone back to the numbers, and Angie breathed a sigh of relief. "Those boxes in your room, maybe."

Of course. Angie gritted her teeth. She was half-tempted to sleep on the sofa, so she never had to go upstairs again. But that was stupid. She went, clomping her heavy boots, up to the room that had once been the house's nursery.

She checked before going in, but the window was still closed, with the box in front of it.

Mum's box was at the bottom of a stack, and Angie was out of breath by the time she unearthed it. She dropped onto the floor, the boards creaking in elderly protest, and pulled on the cardboard flaps until the box came open.

The sketchbook was right on top, as if waiting for her, with its battered green cover so familiar from childhood. Angie eyed it like it was some unidentifiable creature that might or might not be safely dead, but finally she picked it up and opened it.

Dozens of images greeted her eyes. Wiggly outlines of an indeterminate island, changing its shape with every new drawing. Strange birds. Pirates, one with a hook for a hand. An enormous tree, and a ramshackle little house.

A boy, slender with youth and wild with energy, again and

again. The sketches got better as they moved toward the back of the book, but he never had a face, not in any of them. Mum hadn't known what face to give him.

Angie laid the book down and gazed around the room that had been hers since she was little. Mum had insisted on it, just like she had insisted that Dad buy the house when Grandma Marge went into special care, even though they couldn't afford it. Angie still remembered the stories, recited to her like scripture when she was little.

Stories. Just stories.

But what if they weren't?

What if...

The room blurred, its battered shape sliding, obscuring the flaws so badly in need of repair. For a moment, Angie could almost see what it had been, when night-lights burned to keep little children safe.

With the heel of her hand, she wiped away the tears that threatened, and the room solidified once more. She slammed the sketchbook shut and threw it back at the box, not bothering to see if it landed safely before heading for the door.

She gave vent to her feelings on the concrete wall of an abandoned laundrette. The spray paint raked across its surface, spewing out jagged, meaningless lines that weren't words, weren't art, weren't anything. The fumes filled her head and made her giddy.

"Hey! You!"

Angie didn't bother to look in the direction of the shout; she knew what she would see, and looking would only slow her down. Stuffing the canister into her backpack, she took to her heels.

The copper gave chase. New on the job, Angie thought with cynical irritation. Still gets pissed about kids fucking up property. She veered down an alley, hoping to give the pig enough trouble that he'd give up.

No such luck; she heard the footsteps behind her still, the copper shouting for her to stop.

And then from above, she heard a voice crow out.

The triumphant sound, so often described to her, so out of place in the urban landscape of London, took her down like a rugby player. Angie tripped on a broken bit of concrete and went sprawling, ripping out the one good knee of her jeans, taking half the skin off her arm, slamming her chin on the ground. She gasped for air, and when her lungs were working again, she looked back.

The copper had stopped, too, and had his truncheon out, ready to strike the lithe figure between him and Angie. The boy who called himself Peter Pan stood boldly, feet planted wide, and there was a fucking *sword* in his hand. No wonder the truncheon was out.

"Get out of the—" she started to shout at the boy, but as she did so, a brilliant light swooped in and buzzed the rozzer's face. The man shouted and reeled back, swinging the truncheon and missing.

The boy did not miss. He leapt into the air, and it wasn't just a jump: he *hovered*. He flew forward, then struck with his sword.

Angie screamed again and lurched to her feet. The copper dodged, unsuccessfully; the blade didn't skewer him, but it cut deeply into his shoulder. He howled, and over the sound of his pain Angie shrieked, "You can't *stab* him, Jesus Christ, you can't kill a pig, are you *mad?*"

The copper tripped and fell to the pavement. Angie ran forward, not sure what she could do to help him, but she never got the chance to find out; wiry fingers grabbed her wrist, glittery dust showered over her, and then the boy dragged her upwards, into the sky.

"You didn't fly," the boy said after he dropped her onto the grass in Kensington Gardens. He was rubbing his arm, looking offended at having had to drag her weight all the way there. "Don't you know to think happy thoughts?"

"Happy *thoughts?*" Angie could barely get the words out. "Who the *fuck* do you think you are?"

Confusion flitted across his face, ever so briefly. "You know who I am. I'm Peter Pan."

And he was. He crowed; he flew; he showed up in the nursery looking to take little girls to the Neverland. "What if" had become what *was*. The stories were real.

Angie staggered backward and leaned against a tree. "And you've come for me."

Peter brightened immediately. "Yes!"

The insufferable smile on his face did it—the happy, thoughtless assumption that now everything was going the way he wanted, now everything was great.

So he was real. So what?

"Fuck you. I'm not going."

The flickering light zoomed up into Angie's face and made a melodious, glittering sound that somehow managed to be very rude.

Angie swatted at it with her hand. "Go away, you stupid—you stupid *fairy*."

Peter was still staring at her, with the wounded puppy-dog look of a little boy. "But it's time for spring cleaning."

"Spring cleaning?" Angie stared back. "Spring fucking *cleaning*? You've got no clue, do you?"

He drew himself up with overstuffed pride. "Of course I do."

"No. You don't. My mother spent her *whole life* waiting for you. Going to sleep every night in that nursery, hoping she'd wake up to find you there. But you never came, did you? You were off in the Neverland, having fun, and you didn't think about her. You didn't even know she *existed*. I'm not Wendy, you stupid wanker, and I'm not Jane, and I'm not Margaret, either. You took *her* to the Neverland all of twice. She used to tell me about it, you know—before we had to put her in a nursing home, one where they lock the doors and don't let you out. We kept finding her wandering the streets, muttering about 'second to the right.' One time she was out all night, and when they found her just before dawn, she started crying, because they stopped her going straight on till morning."

Angie's breath was coming in great gulping heaves by the time
she ran out of words. The tree was well behind her, and Peter had
retreated before her advance. He had an odd expression on his
face—the expression of someone who sees guilt coming in search
of him, and is trying desperately to pretend he doesn't notice it
while edging very quickly in the other direction. "Time is different
in the Neverland," he said, reluctantly, as if even admitting that
was hard. "And I forget things."

"You forget *people*," Angie said. "We don't matter to you, do
we? You just want someone to come and do your spring cleaning,
and it doesn't matter if it's Grandma Marge or Jane or Wendy,
because it isn't about us; it's about *you*."

"It's about adventure!" Peter protested. "Mermaids, and
Indians, and pirates—"

Angie barked out a laugh. "Pirates? I can get those at the
cinema. I don't need the Neverland. I'm not a kid anymore, and
I'm not going to be your goddamned mother."

Off to the side, where neither of them was watching, the
brilliant light of Tinker Bell sank to the ground, her wings
motionless with shock.

There were tears inside Angie's heart, but the fury was stronger.
It had fed for many years on her resentment, on the memory of
her mother's hopeless patience and her grandmother's fanciful
senility. It had been waiting for this day, even if Angie herself had
never believed it would come. She knew too well the price of that
belief.

"Go away, Peter," Angie said. "We don't want you anymore."

The window rattled, but quietly, as if it did not wish anyone to
notice. The box holding it closed slipped away, sliding along the
old floorboards polished by so many children's feet. The window
blew open, and in came a slender boy, accompanied by a small
light.

The light stayed away from the figure on the bed, feeling none too charitable, and perhaps fearful of waking her. The boy came forward on silent feet and looked down at the girl who lay there: the short, spiked hair, the piercings all along her ears, the mouth set hard even in sleep. Young, but not a child. She did not dream of the Neverland.

He went away a few steps, uncertainly, then sat down on the floor and began to sob.

"Boy, why are you crying?"

A pale figure had sat up in bed. Peter leapt up, wiping away his tears, and made her a courteous bow. "What's your name?" he asked.

"Wendy Moira Angela Darling. What's yours?"

"Peter Pan," he said.

He was an imaginative boy, capable of creating feasts upon which he would glut himself, feasts composed of airy nothings finer than any cook's delicacies. By the power of his imagination, he shaped the world around him, and perhaps he shaped this for himself, out of the memories that so often slipped his mind. Or perhaps this was a ghost, the last, faded remnants of the innocence each girl lost as she grew up and became a woman. She looked a little like Angie, a little like Margaret, a little like Jane…and a great deal like Wendy.

Together they flew out into the nighttime sky, with Tinker Bell coming spitefully along behind, and the window swung itself shut behind them, the box sliding back into place. Peter Pan took his last Wendy to the Neverland, not just for the spring cleaning but forever, and they never came back.

THE GENIUS PRIZE

THERE ARE ABUNDANT RECORDS of the Twentieth Annual Metzger-Patel Genius Prize championship in 2131. Everything from the entry forms for each Contestant Team, to the judges' notes on each creation, to the home videos filmed by proud parents, to the helicopter footage of the aftermath.
Finding out what happened isn't the hard part.
Believing it is.

After the conclusion of the nineteenth championship, Immis Chae interviewed Anjale Metzger for *Globeline*. Metzger and Tahira Patel usually retired out of the public eye after the competition was over, but Patel had given a similar interview after the ninth year, and this time it was Metzger's turn.

"It's become a cliché," the interviewer says in the recording, smiling under the broadcast lights, "but the entries this year really were bigger and better than ever—with an emphasis on bigger. What are you going to do for the twentieth anniversary of the Genius Prize? How are you going to make it stand out, when escalation has become the expected norm for your competition?"

Metzger is less fond of the camera than her wife, but she looks crisp and collected in her tailored silk suit, the grey threading through the black of her mathematically precise cornrows almost more decorative than a sign of age. She does not smile. "Well, Immis, in part that is up to our contestants. It's their creations that the world tunes in to see, and so if those are more impressive every year, that's because these young people keep on coming up with new and more astonishing innovations. But yes, Tahira and I have plans for the twentieth anniversary, just like we did for the tenth. This time we'd like to look back at the history of the prize and honor those who have come before—and that's all I can say for now."

Chae faces the nearest floating camera, and their smile grows wider. "You heard it here, folks: next year you won't just see *one* Genius Prize, but twenty years' worth. I'm sure it will be spectacular."

The camera image from the warehouse in Bamako rocks unsteadily as a parran-alloy arm slams into the wall. "Careful!" Akua Fonghoro shouts, as if her teammate Kisi Abouta is deliberately being careless.

Their mecha staggers drunkenly. "I'm trying!" Kisi shouts back, even though the microphone inside the suit picks up every whisper with perfect clarity. "It's just—this thing—won't—"

The days of simple humanoid shapes are long gone. Everyone knows that Dr. Metzger and her judges score the entries on more than just size, power, agility. Anybody can slap together a mechanical suit, piston-driven arms and legs and a thundering engine to make it go; without style, you're no better than the average middle-class tinkerer in their garage.

The device lurching with a stiff-legged gait toward the cinder-block wall has the head and beak of a skeletal pterosaur, and wings that are extending and retracting in a stuttering rhythm. They aren't used to fly like a bird; no amount of flapping up and down could lift the mass of machinery beneath them, even with modern lightweight alloys. That's what the spinjets are for.

"Breathe," Ye Tangara says from a prudent distance, as one of the spinjets fires briefly, incinerating a stack of fiber rods. "Like you practiced."

Panting comes over the loudspeakers. Kisi manages to turn aside before she runs headfirst into the wall. "Okay. I think I'm getting the hang—"

The left wing shoots out full-force and slams against the

cinderblocks. Kisi's curse is lost within the grinding screech of the collision.

Almost out of frame, she stops the mecha and levers back the top of the pterosaur's skull, exposing her face, which leaks sweat like a crushed sponge. "I swear, I'm going to just rip that thing out of here. We did fine without it before. Why do we need it now?"

"Because," Akua says, as Ye brings Kisi water and mops off her face. "What we've got was good enough to win the Songhali Nationals, but not the Genius Prize. *Everybody* there is going to have a Truong sympathy net. Without one, you won't be able to keep up."

"And with one, I'll fall on my face and be the laughingstock of the world." But Kisi nods away the last of the water and claps her mecha shut again. The machine hums as the sympathy net activates, and the wings rattle shut, unevenly. The loudspeakers pick up her voice again, restored to its usual focus and cool. Nobody lacking in those qualities makes it to the three rounds of the Genius Prize, much less through them.

"I have two months," Kisi says as she stumbles out of the camera's view. "I'll get this."

"God, that stuff stinks."

For all that the robotics teams mock the bioengineers as being "squishy" and not knowing which end of a computer is up, the truth is that the bios know their way around a program or two. They couldn't possibly design their handcrafted genomes, much less produce them, if they didn't.

But it is true that they're more prone to being careless. Chango Benitez used his laptop to call his parents back in Guatemala, and while the camera is off now, he forgot to disable the audio pickup afterward. With enhancement, it's possible to make out his team's entire conversation, right up until the point where Miguel Cobar asks if he remembered to kill the mic and Chango swears, running for his computer.

Before that happens, their team leader and kaiju handler speaks. "I don't care what it smells like, as long as it works." Rico Sarabia's bitter words are undercut by a gagging noise. "Okay, maybe I care a little."

Faint noises register on the mic as he fills the cartridge, loads it into the hypospray, and hooks up the pressure hose. Their organism, a creature best described as an armor-plated, six-armed gorilla with the many-rowed teeth of a shark, is only vulnerable to such a device in one location, but the boys have it well-trained; there is no sound of shuffling, and only a small grunt of complaint, as Rico crawls between its legs, levers up one of the armor plates, and shoots a dose of cutting-edge chemistry into the creature's bloodstream.

"We should have done this months ago," Miguel says as Rico crawls back out. "I can't believe we lost, man. This is our only chance to redeem ourselves."

The Tlachi Institute is the most respected secondary school for biological sciences in the world. They've won fourteen of the last thirty Patel Bioengineering Tournaments, dating back to before the foundation of the Genius Prize. For Rico and his friends to lose the Central American Regional Championships to the Nicaraguan national team was humiliating. Had the Nicaraguans not been disqualified after the fact for outside assistance—a consultation with the leader's aunt at the Shinrasen Center, not covered up quite well enough—Rico, Miguel, and Chango would be staying home this year.

The Tlachi team's chat logs, subpoenaed during the later investigation, reveal that Rico was the one who successfully argued against using obsequium on their kaiju before regionals. Although ruled legal by Dr. Patel and the advisory board of her tournament, he felt the agent was not "in the spirit of things," and preferred to direct his kaiju the old-fashioned way, with shouted commands and hand signals.

He changed his tune after the Nicaraguans' obsequium-dosed three-headed serpent dodged every one of their gorilla's six arms, got it in a pin, and nearly put one head's fangs through its skull.

There's another hypospray hiss on the audio from Chango's laptop as Rico doses himself with dominatio, the companion drug to obsequium. Scruples don't last long in the face of defeat.

Every year, there are new developments. More efficient engines. A carbon nanotube splice that makes the bones lighter and more resilient. Stabilizer systems that mean the mecha spend less time knocking each other over. Fast-coagulating blood. What starts out as secret tech becomes standard military issue, then the plaything of the rich, then fodder for teenagers working in their garages and backyards and high school bio labs.

Many of those things are invented by past winners of the Genius Prize. Some of the new techniques make their debut in the competition. After all, that's why Metzger and Patel founded their respective championships: to encourage innovation, to find and nurture the brightest young minds in their respective fields.

As for why they joined those championships together, pitting the top wonders of each side against one another in a no-holds-barred fighting extravaganza?

They've answered that question a thousand times in a thousand interviews. A polished answer, focus-tested and vetted by lawyers as being non-prosecutable. But Tahira Patel gave the real answer once, when she'd had a bit too much sake at a reception in Tokyo.

"Because it's *fun.*"

What Anjale Meztger meant about history becomes clear during the inaugural parade of the Twentieth Annual Metzger-Patel Genius Prize.

Although not quite as extravagant as the opening ceremonies of the Olympics, the Genius Prize parade is still quite astonishing. For the billions of people worldwide who only tune in to the realms of high school competitive robotics and bioengineering during the third week of June, it's their first chance to see the competitors: massive robots and equally massive kaiju, shaped to look like creations out of science fiction or national folklore or someone's worst nightmare, all stomping or rolling or slithering or flying around the arena where they will soon be demonstrating what they're capable of.

When the masking field drops, revealing the stage at the center of the arena, Metzger and Patel are not alone. Together with the usual array of judges, officials, and security forces, they have the winning entries from the previous nineteen years of both their respective competitions.

The effect is initially comical. In the early days, the standards for what teenagers might be expected to create were a good deal lower than they are today. It is a tradition almost as old as the Genius Prize itself to bemoan the loss of those simpler, more innocent days, before the attention of recruiters and the sizable cash award drove the teams to ever-more ambitious heights. The top mecha from the first year of the competition is little more than human-sized—essentially just a souped-up exoskeleton. The top kaiju from that year isn't even present in person, having died of lung failure six months after the competition. It is represented instead by one of its ninth-generation offspring, having displayed a capacity for budding that surprised its designers as much as anyone else.

But with each subsequent year, the creations get more impressive. Simple human-shaped mecha give way to things with more arms, more legs, more spikes. The kaiju leave nature behind and take hybrid forms even the ancient Greeks never conceived of.

And they get bigger.

A *lot* bigger.

The winners from the previous year—a scythe-armed Cuisinart with no discernible head and a creature that resembles the love child of a squid and a rhinoceros—dwarf Metzger and Patel, towering nearly forty feet tall. The technology for creating such things may fit into a suburban basement, but the creations themselves do not.

So in the end, the effect is exactly as the two women intended. As laughably simple as the early entries may seem, they're the foundation for a progression that has escalated through the years. They make clear the sheer magnitude of what Metzger and Patel have wrought.

In the footage of that evening, there are close-up shots of all the individuals who would become so important a few days later: the Songhali team of Akua, Ye, and Kisi; the Tlachi team of Chango, Miguel, and Rico; the Canadian hacker Tiennot Ahenakew, nearly the only member of his team to survive; Nevali Jones, the head of security for the event; and, in a panning shot across the stands, the Canthorpe twins.

In the focus piece that ran prior to the nineteenth championship, ambition burns within Arthur and Arnold Canthorpe like a flame. You can see it blazing in their eyes, feel the heat of it in every gesture.

"We've been planning this since we were six," Arthur says, slinging one arm around his twin brother. "Eleven years of work. This is the year it's gonna pay off."

From outside the frame, the interviewer asks, "Why did you decide to split up? Why not join forces, work together on the same team? Then you could both win the Genius Prize."

Arnold laughs. "Because we want *all* the prizes. The way we've got it set up, Arthur will win the Metzger Robotics Championship, and I'll win the Patel Bioengineering Tournament. Then we'll face off in the final round, and whoever walks away with the Genius Prize, it'll still be a Canthorpe."

Their confidence is infectious. You can see it in your mind's eye: Arthur Canthorpe holding the robotics trophy, Arnold Canthorpe the one for bioengineering, and between them, the enormous twined helix and gearing of the Genius Prize. The interviewer says, "It's quite a plan. Aren't you competitive with each other at all?"

Arthur laughs. It's indistinguishable from his brother's laugh; their hairstyles are identical, save for the direction of the part. They worked hard to create their public image, the cooperative opposition of the Canthorpe twins. "Oh, sure," he says, and lets go of his brother to punch him gently in the shoulder. "I'm going to kick his—"

Although the courtesy filter transforms his final word to "butt," anyone who reads lips can tell what he really said.

There are no interviews with the twins after their defeat. Although most leaders of losing teams are gracious enough to speak at least briefly with reporters, the Canthorpes left in a fury before the dust had even settled.

Investigators scoured all the records of the first few days of the twentieth competition, not because they were unclear on what happened, but because they wanted to answer the question: could it have been prevented?

The answer, of course, is *yes*. There were countless opportunities for someone to notice what was going on and put a stop to it before the chaos began. But those opportunities all came in the months between the nineteenth and the twentieth competitions— not at the event itself. The government of the Rocky Mountains Federated States, exceedingly eager to pin responsibility for the disaster on as many people as possible, did its very best to flay Nevali Jones alive for being negligent, but the truth is that she wasn't. By the time the various competitors arrived at the stadium outside Aspen that had been chosen to host that year's Genius Prize, there was nothing she could be expected to see, no action she ought to have known to take. Not until the trouble began.

The documents from the investigation describe the first few days as utterly routine, the recordings showing nothing suspicious. Demonstration trials for each of the kaiju, each of the mecha, in alternating turns. The panels of judges inspect them up close, questioning the teams who built or bred them, conducting various tests. Then they back off to a safe distance while the team leaders put their creations through their paces. The robotics pilots climb into their mecha; the bioengineering handlers shepherd their beasts along like proud owners at a dog show. But the differences are visible. With the aid of a Truong sympathy net, the linkage between the mecha pilots and their suits is far more fluid than before, the mechanisms responding to thought instead of controls. With a fresh injection of obsequium rendering them docile, the kaiju almost seem to have a telepathic link with their dominatio-dosed handlers, never hesitating, never balking.

Even knowing what will happen, it's mesmerizing to see. More people tuned in to watch the first round than ever before, just to enjoy the balletic dance of these creations across the arena.

As usual, the judges choose eight in each category to progress to the second round. This is the point at which the whole world starts watching, because who can resist the appeal of watching giant robots slam each other with titanic force, giant beasts tear each other apart? It's better than a movie, because it isn't scripted; it's better than the Olympics, because it's mecha vs. monsters. Metzger and Patel judge this round themselves, basing their choices not simply on the brute question of which entry can beat up the other entries, but on subtleties of movement, speed, elegant engineering.

If there's one downside to the creation of the Genius Prize, it's that it has taken a little of the shine from the awards—the lesser awards, the preliminary awards. People these days use a whole host of deprecatory words to refer to the Metzger Robotics Championship and the Patel Bioengineering Tournament, so thoroughly have they been subsumed into the spectacle of the final round. You can even see it in the faces of the winners, Kisi and her Songhali teammates, Rico and his Tlachi friends: they're happy, of course they're happy, but they're also thinking ahead to the next day. And so are all of the losers, because it's happened before that an entry has lost the individual competition, but won the final prize.

This is where the real fun usually begins, the temptation that led Metzger and Patel to combine their two events into one. The top eight finalists from each category—those still in good enough shape to move, after a night of frantic surgery and repair—march into the arena, for a grand melee of metal against flesh.

In the year 2131, this is when the chaos starts.

There is no footage of how it happened, of course. The Canthorpe twins were far too clever for that. They both placed a close second in their respective competitions, and came near to winning the Genius Prize itself; no one ever accused them of being stupid. They made sure the cameras and microphones where they settled in to work transmitted only what the twins wanted them to.

But it's possible to re-create it from the evidence. Arthur found a security vulnerability in the Truong sympathy net about one month after Truong Industries hired him, and chose not to report this to his employers. Arnold had the more difficult challenge, contaminating an entire production batch of obsequium with a custom-designed virus—and in fact, one of the kaiju entries was dosed from an earlier batch, and failed to be suborned as expected.

Every single recording of the main event agrees: precisely thirty seconds into the melee, the twins take over.

Fifteen of the titanic figures thudding and whirring and flying toward one another across the huge arena stagger to a halt. The sixteenth, the French scorpion that has escaped the trap, pulls up short a moment later; its handler has noticed the sudden stillness, and thinks someone has given a signal to abort the competition.

In unison, the fifteen under Canthorpe control wheel to face the box from which Metzger and Patel are watching. Every loudspeaker in the arena, every mecha's external output, and quite a few personal devices that have been insufficiently shielded, suddenly boom out the identical voices of Arthur and Arnold Canthorpe, speaking in eerie (and pre-recorded) unison.

"Peoples of the world," the twins declare into the growing silence. "Last year, Anjale Metzger and Tahira Patel judged our creations inferior. Insufficient. Unworthy of their respective awards, and of the Genius Prize itself. They judged *us* unworthy. We have come here today to show them—to show all of you—how wrong they were."

The French handler, Amina Beausoleil, breaks the stillness. Her scorpion wheels and charges the nearest kaiju.

Some people later claim that Amina thought she could win the Genius Prize while everyone else's backs were quite literally turned. But with eight mecha and seven kaiju under Canthorpe control, she had to know her creature didn't stand a chance. Footage from a thousand angles shows the scorpion spitting a tangling web at the legs at the Greater Irish kaiju that sends it crashing to the ground, but Japan's teddy-bear-shaped mecha breathes fire that crisps the web into ash—fire-breathing still being popular for its visual effect, even though it's easy to engineer and useless against any competitive creation. The whip arm of the Brazilian mecha duels briefly with the scorpion's extendable tail, but three seconds later it's over. A camera in one of the exit tunnels from the field shows that Amina abandoned her charge the instant the rest of the entries turned on her beast, running for cover—an action that certainly saved her life.

During this brief fight, one of the mecha begins to spasm. Then another, then another, until all of them have twitched and then fallen still.

Only when that is done do they turn against their surroundings, unleashing their firepower on the shielded stands that surround them.

Credit goes to the Songhali team for observing appropriate safety standards, and installing a purely mechanical hatch release in their pterosaur. Thanks to this, Kisi is able to pop open her construct and dive free after Arthur takes it over. Not all of the other pilots were as diligent, and so they remain trapped, helpless passengers in their own creations, as the Canthorpe twins begin to wreak vengeance for what they saw as their unfair defeat the previous year.

The teammates of the pilots, and all of the kaiju engineers, are on the field. They know first-hand exactly how destructive their creations can be. A few of them waste precious seconds trying to regain control; others realize the futility, and begin fleeing immediately.

Nevali Jones is in the judges' box with Metzger and Patel at the start of the attack. Her body cam shows the first rocket exploding against the front window, and (contrary to those who would like to accuse her of negligence or incompetence) less than two seconds go by before she takes action. The judges' box is defended, of course, because accidents have happened before. But anything that offers visibility to the outside world has certain innate vulnerabilities against focused attack, and so you can hear Jones shouting for Metzger, Patel, and their various guests to retreat to the much more heavily fortified chamber behind. She covers their retreat herself, even though frail flesh isn't much of a shield against a kaiju or a mecha; her own body armor is only rated to resist threats up to Hellstop rockets, Class B plasma drills, and fluoroantimonic acid.

Once the dignitaries are secured, she descends to the arena below, shouting orders to her subordinates as she goes.

Chango, as the Tlachi team's tactical coordinator, had a drone circling the field so he could advise Rico in handling their kaiju. Its auto-tether drags it after him when he and a dozen others retreat into one of the tunnels, and so unlike most of the drones in the air when the Canthorpes took over, it escapes the destruction outside long enough to memorialize what comes next.

The shot is from above, but the figures are recognizable. From the Tlachi team, Chango and Rico; Miguel has escaped, but via a different tunnel. From the Songhali team, Kisi, Akua, and Ye. From the Canadian team, Tiennot; all three members of the Brazilian team; two from the Pakistani team; from the Sinai team, Muhammed Najjar, badly injured by shrapnel; and Yankton Robins, an arena employee responsible for supplying food to the kaiju.

Akua immediately begins applying first aid to Muhammed. Most of the others are shouting in a medley of languages; isolation analysis later teases out their words, the majority of which are profanities supposedly unsuitable to their tender years. Then Kisi's voice rises above them all. (Her words, and most of the subsequent conversations, are in Kotava.) "What the hell is going on out there?"

The Canthorpes' message is still broadcasting. Despite the noise from outside, it echoes through the tunnel in which the group shelters.

"Who else has the capacity to hijack the sympathy nets in all the mecha built by the newest crop of supposed geniuses?" the twins boast. "Who else can brainwash kaiju that supposedly answer to no one but their handlers? The display of coordination and skill you see before you now—"

"What fucking coordination?" Kisi yells toward the mouth of the tunnel. The flames consuming that end of the field are not visible in the drone's view, but their light dances across the huddled figures. "You're destroying everything!"

Tiennot stands up from his crouch against the wall. "Listen to the message! The ambient sound—it's pre-recorded, not live. I don't think this was supposed to happen."

Rico answers him with a well-chosen vulgarity in Spanish, then says, "Who cares what was supposed to happen? There are people dead out there!"

(At the moment he says it, the death toll stands at thirty-four, all individuals who were on the field when this began. It will climb fast as the stadium's shielding begins to fail.)

Tiennot's hands flap in the air, beating out a swift rhythm as his mind focuses on the problem. "The sympathy nets. He hijacked them—must have been Arthur. But one mind can't control eight at once. He must have daisy-chained them together, so that he's controlling one and that controls the next and so on—but that only works if he can maintain the focus necessary to stop sensory input from washing back through the chain. Did you see them spasm? He must have let that slip on the first link.

Then he'd be hit by the second, and his odds of resisting that are lower, so—"

He doesn't finish the sentence, but he doesn't have to. The image of dominoes falling is so clear, it might as well be on the video feed.

Chango and Rico are kaiju crafters. They've never worked with sympathy nets. "What does that *mean?*" Rico demands.

Kisi slams her hand against the wall. "It means Arthur Canthorpe has gone insane. Taking all the mecha with him."

"What about that *comemierdas* Arnold?" Chango says, gesticulating wildly toward the tunnel entrance. "What's his excuse?"

An explosion cuts short any answer the others might have given. The shock wave knocks Chango's drone into a wall, destroying it. The next record of this group comes from inside the west loading dock, whose security barriers Tiennot has hacked. By this point Akua has taken Muhammed toward Infirmary Station D, and two of the Brazilians, along with Yankton Robins, have chosen to flee into the surrounding mountains, hoping to find safety there. Thanks to Robins, all three will make it to Aspen, the nearest town. Others who try the same escape do not fare so well.

"We've got to do something," Rico says. "We can't just let a pair of insane losers rampage around with kaiju and mecha—*our* kaiju and mecha." He says that last part with venomous fury.

"What do you think we can do?" Ye asks wildly. "Throw wrenches at them? Carve them apart with welding torches? We built ours to be indestructible!"

One of the Pakistanis says, "The contest authorities have their own kaiju and mecha—"

"Which also use sympathy nets," Tiennot says, with bitter amusement.

Chango nods. "And obsequium, I'm sure. They have all the best tech before we do, unless we invent it ourselves."

Ye snorts. "Right. So all we have to do is invent some brand new bit of tech out of whatever we've got in our pockets."

While all of this is going on, Kisi drifts a few steps away from the group. At first her posture is limp and hopeless, her movements dazed. But as Ye speaks, she straightens, her gaze going into the distance.

"No," Kisi says, not looking at any of them. "Not something new."

In the tunnels under the arena stands, Nevali Jones is hunting Canthorpes.

They have prepared for this, of course. She's already walked into several booby traps, not because she failed to see them before they triggered, but because she cannot afford to take the time to disarm them. Instead she trusts in her armor. It is now blackened and smoldering, the silencers destroyed, such that each step she takes clangs against the concrete floor.

The final defense is a good deal subtler. It has been growing for weeks, seeded by Arnold Canthorpe via an "accidental" spill the janitor did not realize should have been cleaned with hydrochloric acid.

By the time Nevali Jones walks into it, the creature has grown to coat the hallway in something that will pass for concrete, if you don't stab it to see if it will bleed.

It's smart, too. It lets her get halfway down the hall, halfway to the door of the generator room where the Canthorpes are holed up, before it moves.

Then the entire corridor comes to life and closes in on her like a fist.

Tiennot throws the switch in the west loading dock. The lights come on in rows, a gunfire volley of illumination rattling from the near end to the far, revealing in true color what, until that point, had been recorded only in infrared.

The mecha stand silent along one wall. The cages facing them from the other wall are quiet only because there are sound dampeners on each one; Metzger and Patel wanted all attention on the new entries for the Genius Prize, not the old ones. But they're there: kaiju and the descendants of kaiju, and the mecha they once battled.

"You've got to be kidding me," Chango says in Spanish, before collecting his wits and switching back to Kotava. "None of those things can stand up to what's out there!"

"They're all we've got," Kisi says. "And they don't have sympathy nets or obsequium."

Ye utters an oath in Igbo and runs down the line to the robotic winner from six years before. "He's here! Anansi is here!"

The construct in front of her can only be called a spider as a courtesy toward its eight legs; unlike the French scorpion that died on the field a little while ago, it does not spin webs. But its Nigerian creators named it for the famous West African spider god, and so that is the name by which the world knows it. Although the two countries have been longtime rivals, Songhali robotics students have a great deal of respect for Anansi, whose sheer agility and ability to climb larger mecha to find a better angle of attack made for a thrilling display in 2125.

"Do you even know how to pilot that thing?" Chango demands.

Kisi doesn't look at him. All her attention is on Anansi. "I've watched the recordings of the Nigerians. We tried building our own six-legged mecha a few years ago—couldn't resolve some center of gravity issues with the weaponry. But that won't be a problem here."

Meanwhile, Rico is studying the various kaiju. Nine of them are Tlachi creations, the legacy of a long tradition of victorious teams. His gaze lights on the 2128 winner: La Diestra, who resembles nothing so much as a deinonychus the size of a tyranno-saurus rex. She, too, is memorable—albeit for a different reason.

Tiennot makes a sound like he choked on his tongue. "You can't be serious."

"What choice do we have?" Rico asks.

The ensuing silence breaks Kisi's attention away from Anansi. Her gaze meets Rico's. Then she says, "Oh."

Finally Rico says, "We need more than just us."

Kisi nods and faces the Pakistanis. "You in?" She doesn't even wait for their answer before she adds, "Ye, round up anybody you can find. Pilots, handlers—anybody brave enough to try. But hurry."

Outside, the destruction is mounting.

The recruiter for the Shinrasen Center left his standing camera rig in his private box. The various explosions have shaken it out of its original alignment, leaving it pointed at the mouth of one of the tunnels—the one nearest to the west loading dock.

It records, with astonishing clarity, the moment when the tide turns.

Rico charges out first, mounted bareback atop La Diestra. The huge, dinosaurian kaiju—the only one ever to win while carrying her handler—provides cover for fast-moving Anansi, whose faceted pilot bubble refracts the face of Kisi, bellowing a war cry. Behind them comes a herd of other mecha and kaiju, winners of the previous competitions, piloted and directed by more than a dozen brave contestants.

It is the grandest grand melee the Genius Prize has ever seen. Anansi swarms up the back of the Canadian grizzly-shark and blows open the hatch; two legs reach in, snag Tiennot's compatriot Miigwan, and drop her to the waiting arms of a small naga kaiju below. Rico on La Diestra kites several of the Canthorpes' enslaved mecha around the field, and one of them falls into a pit dug by the infamous Tlachi-crafted Mole Man from the 2117 competition. (He is not under anyone's control; he is simply burrowing for the sheer joy of it, as he does whenever given access to dirt.) Anansi leaps from the grizzly-shark across to the Lovecraftian monstrosity the Norwegians brought, then leaps again just as the Japanese teddy bear breathes fire across its supposed ally. The Holy Angel of 2120 defends a large portion of the stands, where the collapsing structure has trapped several thousand spectators.

Chango was right. Very few of the previous winners can hope

to stand up against the most recent entries; even Anansi and La Diestra are outmatched. But the young people who have taken the field can and do save lives, covering the evacuation of the stadium, and giving the crazed Canthorpes something to focus on other than mass slaughter.

And Kisi manages more. When three of Anansi's legs are crushed by her own pterodactyl, leaving that construct helpless on the field, she doesn't hesitate. She leaves the pilot's compartment and climbs the pterodactyl's leg while it finishes smashing the Nigerian spider. Like most mecha, it's built to tackle things its own size; it can't grab Kisi, and has no weaponry it can point so close to its own body. When she arrives under its jaw, Arthur Canthorpe can't even see her on the mecha's external sensors.

The Songhali team installed the sympathy net only after their national championships. It's an add-on, not integrated into the frame the way it would have been had they built it in from the start.

Ye's toolbelt is around Kisi's waist. Clinging to the outside of the pterodactyl even as it turns its attention to the rest of the field, she removes the panel on the underside of its jaw and shorts out the sympathy net. The pterodactyl stops dead.

The hatch is still open, left that way during Kisi's earlier escape. She climbs back inside, and as the spinjets fire and the pterodactyl takes flight, the interior mic picks up her next words.

"I'll show you who's a genius."

The lens of Nevali Jones' body cam is smeared with blood and ectoplasm, but it still shows the furious, horrified, defiant face of Arnold Canthorpe when she blows the door off its hinges, and the twitching body of Arthur Canthorpe on the floor, overwhelmed by the sensory input of too many sympathy nets at once.

She doesn't bother with speech. She just stuns Arnold, then Arthur, and then shoots them both again for good measure.

On the field above, the remaining enemy mecha stop. The

remaining enemy kaiju stagger and fall.

The arena is silent, except for the crackle of fire, and then the agonizing, metallic screech of La Diestra finishing what she started: tearing the arm off the Japanese teddy bear.

Wheeling overhead, the Songhali pterodactyl lets out a victorious cry.

Out of respect for the dead, there was no competition in 2132.

Metzger and Patel gave no personal interviews during that time. They testified before judges and committees, gave public statements, and spoke privately with the families of those who had lost loved ones. They donated enormous sums to charity. And they made sure the heroes of the day were honored as they deserved, from Nevali Jones down to Yankton Robins and an arena janitor who led fleeing spectators to the shelter of a supply closet—anyone who helped save lives. Kisi Abouta and Rico Sarabia were named the joint winners of the Genius Prize: the first time the award was given to two individuals from separate teams.

They shared the cash with everyone who had helped them that day.

A little over one year after the disaster, Metzger and Patel appeared together on Immis Chae's show. After a brief review of the previous year's tragedy, Chae cuts straight to the question on everyone's mind.

"Will the Genius Prize continue?"

Patel glances at Metzger and says, "My wife and I still believe in the principles that led us to create our respective competitions, and the Genius Prize itself. But it's undeniable that the entries have grown far beyond anything we envisioned when we started out."

"And with that," Metzger says, "the danger has grown as well."

Chae says, "So you plan to end it?"

It's a sensible idea, but you can hear the disappointment in their voice. Metzger smiles. "Not exactly. We'll be back in 2133…"

"…but we'll be taking it in a different direction," Patel finishes. In unison, they reach into their pockets and set two objects on the table before them, neither more than three inches tall. "Miniaturization."

AFTERWORD

One of the things I love about urban fantasy is the way it runs counter to certain assumptions. For ages we've had this idea that magic and technology don't mix: the former belongs to Ye Olde Mediaevalle Societies, while the latter belongs to us. That idea dates back to at least the Victorian period, when the fairies were said to be "flitting" from England because of scientific progress and the Industrial Revolution, and Sir James George Frazer opined that humanity inevitably progressed from magic to religion to science (leaving the earlier stages behind as it went); for all I know, it goes further back still.

But Frazer was—how shall I phrase this—*full of it*. People don't give up magic to believe in religion, or give up religion to believe in science. And technology and magic can co-exist in the same story. The entire sub-genre of urban fantasy is proof of that. Stories about magic are a way of inscribing an extra layer of meaning onto the world we live in; I doubt we'll ever grow out of that.

I've written urban fantasy short fiction that isn't contained in this collection. Several of my retellings (stories directly based on folklore sources) fit in the genre perfectly well. I could have put them in this book; I only held off because I intend to do two collections of retellings, one themed around folksongs, the other around mythology and folklore. I prefer not to duplicate content between these collections, so my urban fantasy works are to some extent going to be spread across multiple volumes.

That's it for my general remarks. For commentary on the individual stories, read on.

STORY NOTES

NOTES ON "COYOTAJE"

After Ekaterina Sedia edited a werewolf anthology (*Running With the Pack*, about which more in a later note), she decided to do a sequel of sorts, covering shapeshifters who turned into animals other than wolves. But I cannot in any way call this story a sequel to "Comparison of Efficacy Rates," the story I wrote for that first anthology, because ye *gods*, they could not be more dissimilar in tone. And, for that matter, in protagonist. The unnamed biologist from "Comparison of Efficacy Rates" has a complete lack of consideration for her fellow human beings. Inés is much more ethical.

When I asked myself what other animal I might like to write about, my thoughts immediately headed for cats. It could have been a housecat (one of my discarded ideas for *Running With the Pack* was a cat who had been bitten by a werewolf and wanted to die of shame), but a big predator would probably work better, like a jaguar—

—and that easily, I had my story. I knew of *nagualismo*, a kind of indigenous Mexican sorcery that revolves around animal spirits and shapeshifters, from my previous research into Mesoamerica (which also gave me "A Mask of Flesh," collected in *Maps to Nowhere*, and "La Molejera" in this volume). And if I was writing about Mexican shapeshifters, well, the term "coyote" was just sitting there, waiting for me to do something with it. Thus was born "Coyotaje," a story named for the practice of smuggling undocumented immigrants across the U.S.-Mexico border.

One of the things I love about writing fiction for a living is that it gives me a push to learn about things I might otherwise leave untouched. For example, that kind of immigration: the methods, the risks, the official responses and the unofficial ones, positive and negative alike. And the way the border divides a world—because it isn't really the U.S. on one side and Mexico on the other, a sharp transition; people on both sides have ties of family and culture across the line. The situation is much more complicated than I could encompass in a single short story, but I know more about it than I did before, and I'm glad of that.

Unfortunately, in the years since I first wrote this story, the immigration situation in the United States has gotten substantially more dire than what's depicted here. It's depressing when you realize your fictional villains are much less callous and cruel than people in the real world. I devoutly hope that it will improve, such that people reading this story in the future encounter it with a much better situation in mind.

"Coyotaje" was originally published in *Running With the Pack*, edited by Ekaterina Sedia, in April 2011.

NOTES ON "SELECTION"

In a way, I owe Stephenie Meyer (the author of the *Twilight* series) a thank-you for this story. I was thinking about the vampires in her world—you know, the sparkly kind—and how her story sporadically attempts to insist on the angst of being a vampire, despite having removed pretty much every drawback to *being* a vampire that usually attends the concept. I mean, heck. With all the advantages that kind of vampirism brings...who *wouldn't* want to be one? They'd have so many people clamoring to be turned, they'd need an application process.

The resulting story is one of the more stylistically weird things I've ever written (at least at the time of publishing this collection). It began with the first line and snowballed from there, one weird detail after another. Is there a logic behind them? Maybe. But maybe in places the logic is just, "let's see what we can convince people to do."

After all, nobody said these vampires were *nice*.

"Selection" was originally published in issue #13 of *Electric Velocipede*, in November 2007.

Notes on "Such as Dreams Are Made Of"

The first *Cirque du Soleil* act I think I ever saw was "Banquine," from the show *Quidam* (and also seen, in slightly different form, in the film *Journey of a Man*). To this day, it remains one of my favorites. There are no props involved: just a troupe of men and women engaging in phenomenal acrobatics, their bodies painted concrete grey or bone white. The moment I saw them, I thought, *this is what it looks like when a city comes to life.*

Greek mythology had nymphs inhabiting trees, rivers, mountains. Why not buildings? Why not things of the modern, urban world?

To date, this is the only story I've published that grew from that original idea. There may be more someday, though. I quite like the idea that urban fantasy isn't just about creatures from agrarian folktales persisting into the current day; it can also be about magic arising from the modern world we live in.

"Such as Dreams Are Made Of" was originally published in issue #8 of *Aberrant Dreams*, in summer 2006.

Notes on "La Molejera"

In the notes for my story "A Mask of Flesh" (collected in *Maps to Nowhere*), I described how I took an undergraduate folklore seminar that introduced me to Mesoamerican folklore and mythology. When I finally got around to doing the class reading—years after the fact, I'm embarrassed to admit—I was particularly struck by the way it described multiple worlds and multiple apocalypses before our current time began...and how humanity was made from the ground-up bones of previous creatures, mixed with the blood of the gods, given in sacrifice to create life.

Because I was in graduate school for anthropology when I got the idea, it was only natural for me to approach this through the lens of a grad student working on her dissertation, discovering Cihuacoatl grinding bones in the forest, preparing for the end of this world. I owe an enormous debt of gratitude to Alan Sandstrom's *Corn Is Our Blood: Culture and Ethnic Identity in a Contemporary Aztec Indian Village*, which is the source of pretty much all of my detail on life in the fictional village of Chalchihuitlan. (Yes, I read a four-hundred-page ethnography in order to write an 8500-word story.) The translation of the "Legend of the Suns" is excerpted from John Bierhorst's *History and Mythology of the Aztecs: The Codex Chimalpopoca.* I also have to thank Kier Salmon, who assisted me with research and Nahuatl orthography.

Needless to say, everything involving La Molejera (severing the long bones, the feather-boy, etc.) is invented for this story. The other details of life in the Huasteca Veracruzana are probably out of date by this point in time, as *Corn Is Our Blood* came out in 1992, but I have made them as accurate as I can.

"La Molejera" was originally published in the Fall 2019 issue of *Cirsova Magazine* in September 2019.

Notes on "Comparison of Efficacy Rates for Seven Antipathetics As Employed Against Lycanthropes"

I said in my notes on the previous story that "Selection" is one of the most stylistically weird things I've written to date. To date, this is the only piece that gives it a run for its money.

Credit for this one goes to the late Michael Briggs, husband of the urban fantasy novelist Patricia Briggs. The html link in the story is real; assuming it hasn't broken by the time you read this, the address will take you to a page on her site, which is his lengthy tale of attempting to forge silver bullets. Short form is, *it's really bloody difficult.* Silver has a fairly high melting point (no tossing

Grandma's crucifix onto a campfire and pouring bullets out a couple of minutes later), and it's prone to cooling in a way that leaves imperfections in the final product—imperfections that will at a minimum throw off your aim, and possibly even jam your gun.

So if silver bullets don't work...what does?

Ask a question like that, get a story like this. At least if you're me.

"Comparison of Efficacy Rates" (as I generally call it, because the full title is way too long to say all the time) was originally published in *Running With the Pack*, ed. Ekaterina Sedia, in April 2010.

NOTES ON "THE LAST WENDY"

This story was born out of listening to a friend present a paper at the International Conference on the Fantastic in the Arts many years ago. The topic of the paper was the changing representation of Peter in *Peter Pan* adaptations—aging him up from a little boy "who still had all his first teeth" to a borderline-sexy teenager— but toward the end of her paper, my friend made a throwaway comment about how the novel ends, where it says that after Wendy was too old Peter came back for her daughter Jane, and then for Jane's daughter Margaret.

The phrase "the last Wendy" popped into my head, and refused to leave.

But the story itself took much longer. I wrote the beginning almost immediately, with Peter coming into the nursery in the modern world and Angie not behaving at all like he expected. After that, though, it stalled out. Until one Christmas I was chatting with my sister about the story, and in the middle of that I found myself saying, "I think...I'm trying to force it to have a happy ending. What if I made it cynical instead?"

And my sister said, "That's horrible. You should do it."

See, my original conception for the story was some kind of

uplifting thing about Angie finding wonder here in the real world instead of having to run away to the Neverland for it. Maybe creating her own crew of "Lost Boys" or whatever. Which ordinarily is the kind of thing I'm all for; like I said in my Afterword, I resist the idea that the modern world must be flat and banal.

But…this wasn't that story. Because buried underneath the treacly surface of *Peter Pan* as you're used to thinking of it is this really dark edge: Peter is actually a little sociopath. As many children his age are; if he still has all his first teeth, he can't be more than maybe six. When the Lost Boys shoot down the Wendy-bird and Peter thinks she's dead, he doesn't grieve or get angry at them—he goes sidling away like he can't be blamed if he pretends he never saw the body. He forgets about Wendy for long enough that she grows up and has a daughter, and we have no reason to think he wouldn't forget about Jane, too, and all the rest of them.

With that bitter edge in there, I couldn't wrestle this story around to be about how Angie finds happiness and wonder on her own. It's about the damage Peter did, and what happens when that damage makes somebody reject wonder entirely.

"The Last Wendy" was originally published in issue #81 of *On Spec*, in the summer of 2010.

NOTES ON "THE GENIUS PRIZE"

In addition to writing short fiction and novels, I've done some work for role-playing games. Primarily that's been for various editions of *Legend of the Five Rings*, but I've also written micro-settings for several of the Tiny d6 games: brief descriptions of a scenario suited to the game in question, with plot hooks GMs can use to get the ball rolling.

The second one I wrote was for an expansion of the *Tiny Frontiers* science fiction game, called *Mecha vs. Monsters*. The concept behind the game was the "giant robots fighting kaiju" subgenre, seen in films like *Pacific Rim* and the *Neon Genesis Evangelion* anime…which is one that, between you and me, I'm very hit-or-miss with. A good enough story will pull me in, but the simple premise of those things smashing together doesn't do a lot for me. So how was I to come up with a micro-setting for it? And then I thought of high school robotics competitions. And then I thought of the possibility that someday we'll have a biological equivalent.

The micro-setting was called "The Grand Prize" instead of "The Genius Prize," but the core concept was still there: Anjale Metzger and Tahira Patel's joint tournament, pitting mecha vs. kaiju, and something going horribly, horribly wrong. When I got invited to submit a story for a kaiju anthology, working with the same company, I leapt at the chance to play with this idea some more. Writing the story version was huge amounts of fun; most of what I write is much more restrained, me trying to make things fit into the bounds of plausibility and logic somehow—but with this one I basically ripped the brakes out of the car and threw them out the window. Who cares if any of the science here makes sense? The ridiculousness of it is the *point*. I wrote it all in a mad rush, and the ending line fell into place with a click.

Is it urban fantasy? Not really, except insofar as the "science" here is made from Grade A Swiss cheese and might as well be magic. But this story fits better into my urban fantasy collection than any of the others, so here it is, tucked in at the end where maybe nobody will notice.

"The Genius Prize" was originally published in *Kaiju Rising II: Reign of Monsters*, ed. N.X. Sharps and Alana Abbott, in the fall of 2018.

About the Author

MARIE BRENNAN is a former anthropologist and folklorist who shamelessly pillages her academic fields for inspiration. She most recently misapplied her professors' hard work to *The Night Parade of 100 Demons*, a *Legend of the Five Rings* novel, and *The Mask of Mirrors*, the first book of the Rook and Rose trilogy (jointly written with Alyc Helms as M.A. Carrick). Her Victorian adventure series The Memoirs of Lady Trent was a finalist for the Hugo Award; the first book of that series, *A Natural History of Dragons*, was a finalist for the World Fantasy Award. Her other works include the Doppelganger duology, the urban fantasy Wilders series, the Onyx Court historical fantasies, the Varekai novellas, and nearly sixty short stories, as well as the *New Worlds* series of worldbuilding guides. For more information, visit swantower.com, her Twitter @swan_tower, or her Patreon at www.patreon.com/swan_tower.

ABOUT BOOK VIEW CAFÉ

Book View Café Publishing Cooperative (BVC) is an author-owned cooperative of professional writers, publishing in a variety of genres such as fantasy, romance, mystery, and science fiction.

BVC authors include New York Times and USA Today best-sellers; Nebula, Hugo, and Philip K. Dick Award winners; World Fantasy Award and Campbell Award nominees; and winners and nominees of many other publishing awards.

Since its debut in 2008, BVC has gained a reputation for producing high-quality e-books, and is now bringing that same quality to its print editions.

Made in the USA
Las Vegas, NV
21 March 2022

46063370R00080